Cosmic Crime Stories
April 2025

Edited by Tyree Campbell

*

Cosmic Crime Stories
April 2025
Edited by Tyree Campbell

Cover art "Serve and Protect" by Brian Quinn
Cover design by Marcia A. Borell

First Printing April 2025
Hiraeth Publishing
http://hiraethsffh.com/
@HiraethPublish1

Visit http://hiraethsffh.com/ for online science fiction, fantasy, horror, scifaiku, and more. Also visit the Hiraeth Publishing bookstore for paperbacks, magazines, anthologies, and chapbooks. Support the small, independent press...

Contents

Novelettes

Short Stories

Illustrations

Iuliae: Past Tense
By Tyree Campbell

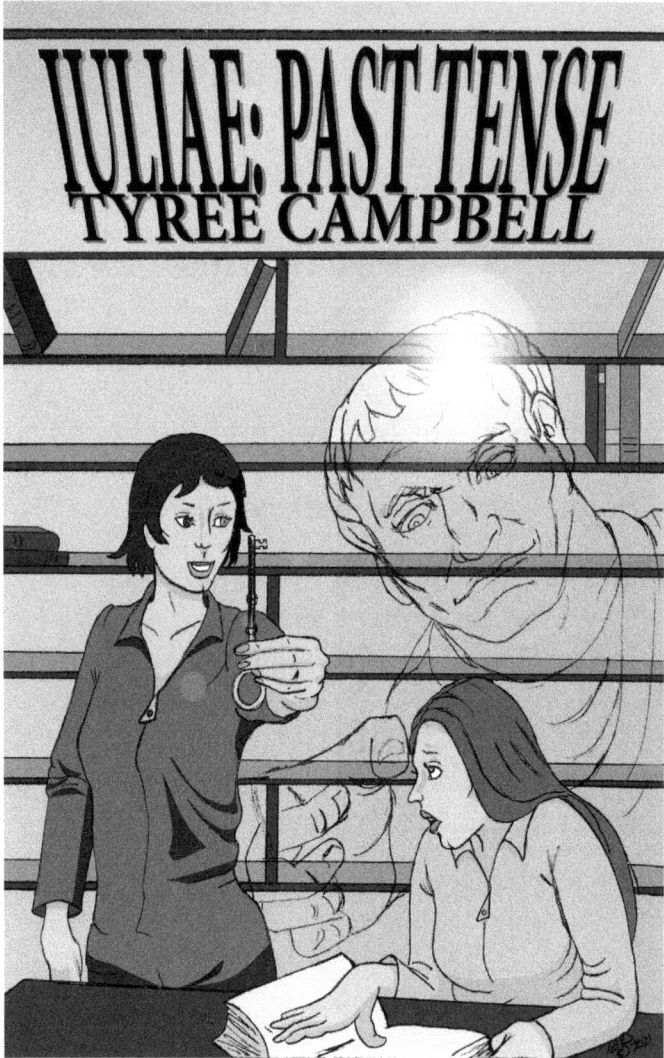

Two sisters of the Iulius Family have run away from the restrictions and rules of their settlement on a remote world, and embark on a journey of discovery, to learn what to do with their new-found freedom. Along the way, they become smugglers, and opponents of human trafficking, and become fugitives from the law and from the corporations.

Iulia Sexta, the younger of the two sisters, is suffering from an identity crisis. Is it gender dysphoria? Was she supposed to be a man? Is that why she likes girls? Or is a ghost from one of her previous lives now trying to haunt his way back into the living by taking over her body and mind?

With both the past and the present pursuing them, Iulia Tertia and Iulia Sexta find their future under constant attack. Doing the right thing is not only difficult at best, but may well result in their deaths. What to do? One thing at a time...

https://www.hiraethsffh.com/product-page/iuliae-past-tense-by-tyree-campbell

A Little Help, Please

In the world of the small indie press we fight a never-ending battle for attention to our work, as writers and in publishing. Here's an example: big publishers [you know who they are] have gobs of $$$ that they can devote to advertising and marketing. Here at Hiraeth Publishing, our advertising budget consists of the deposits for whatever soda bottles and aluminum cans we can find alongside the highways. Anti-littering laws make our task even more difficult . . . ☺

That's where YOU come in. YOU are our best promoter. YOU are the one who can tell others about us. Just send 'em to our website, tell them about our store. That's all. Just that.

Of course, we don't mind if you talk us up. We're pretty good, you know. We have some award-winning and award-nominated writers and artists, plus other voices well-deserving to be heard [not everyone wins awards, right?] but our publications are read-worthy nevertheless.

That number once again is:

www.hiraethsffh.com

Friend us on Facebook at Hiraeth Publishing
Follow us on Twitter at @HiraethPublish1

The Neighbor
Alice Baburek

Alice Baburek

All the lawns on Mentone Avenue are mowed on Wednesdays. But this particular Wednesday, Willie Ashbluff's lawn remained untouched. Along with the overgrown bushes along the front of his house that begged for attention. Willie's neighbor, Derek Windward, noticed the absence of his friend. It had been days since he saw Willie leave for work on Monday morning. They had waved to one another, along with giving a "Good morning" shout.

And now it was Sunday. Derek moved the blind on the window that faced his friend's house. Willie's Chevy Silverado sat silent in the driveway. It was unlike Willie to let his yard go unkempt.

Derek snagged his cell phone off the marbled kitchen counter. He hit redial to Willie's phone. Unexpectedly, he got Willie's voicemail, only to find out it was full. No further messages could be left. Without hesitation, Derek called the non-emergency number to the police.

"Cedar Rapids Police," announced the dispatcher.

"Hello...my name is Derek Windward, and I live on Mentone Avenue. My neighbor, Willie Ashbluff...and he's my friend, too...well, I haven't seen him in about six days. I was wondering if maybe you could send an officer out to conduct a welfare check on Willie?"

"Are you sure Mr. Ashbluff is not on vacation or left for a few days?" asked the dispatcher.

"I guess...I guess it could be possible, but his truck is sitting in his driveway. I don't know how he would go anywhere without it," said Derek.

He began to pace back and forth across his living room. His heart raced. He should have called sooner. Something was wrong with Willie. He could feel it.

"Please...just send an officer to check on Willie. The address is four two three seven Mentone Avenue," said Derek.

"Mr. Windward, we will send out an officer as soon as possible," replied the female officer.

"Thank you."

Derek disconnected the call. Once again, he glanced out his window. The evening was drawing near. A slight shiver ran down his spine. Something was definitely wrong.

It was almost midnight when the Cedar Rapids Police Department cruiser pulled into Willie's driveway. Two police officers, a tall, muscular male and short petite female, flashed their lights on the truck in the driveway. Both officers peered inside.

Derek jumped up when he heard the car. He rushed out the front door to greet the officers with a few swift steps across the grass. Both cops quickly turned and centered their flashlights directly into his face.

"I'm...I'm the one who called...Derek Windward. I'm a friend of Willie Ashbluff," he explained while holding his hand in front of his eyes to deflect the blinding lights.

"Do you have your ID?" asked the female officer.

Derek pulled out a wallet from his back pocket and handed her his driver's license. She snatched it and gave it a quick glance, then handed it back to him.

"Mr. Windward, when was the last time you saw Mr. Willie Ashbluff?" questioned the male officer. He was still looking inside the empty Silverado.

"Like I told the dispatcher when I called...Monday morning. We were both leaving for work and gave a wave. I haven't seen him since. I tried calling, but his voicemail box is full, which is highly irregular since he has no family and very few friends. Why would his voicemail be full?" asked Derek. "It doesn't make sense."

"Mr. Windward, please stay here," insisted the male cop.

Both officers moved to Willie's side door and proceeded to bang loudly on it.

"Mr. Ashbluff...this is the Cedar Rapids Police. Please open the door," shouted the male cop.

The house sat dark and silent. They pounded harder, to no avail.

"Let's check to see if we can gain access," said the female officer to her partner.

The tall officer gave a slight nod. They flashed their lights up and down Willie's house, then disappeared around back.

Derek shifted his feet. He was sweating, even though the night air was brisk. He should have been cold with just a long-sleeved flannel and jeans. But he wasn't. He knew in his gut it was going to be bad. Real bad.

Minutes felt like hours. Finally, the two officers returned. One was speaking into his shoulder com.

"Mr. Windward. We'd like you to come down to the station. We have a few more questions, if you don't mind," asked the tall cop.

"Did you get in? Did you find Willie? Is he all right?" Derek looked back and forth between the two officers.

"We'd like you to come down to the station." The female officer opened the back door of the police cruiser. "Mr. Windward...take a seat," she insisted.

Derek ran his shaky hand through his thick hair. As he slowly got into the cruiser, an unmarked car pulled up in front of Willie's home. Two dark suited men got out.

"Around back, Detectives, we secured the scene." The female officer slammed the cruiser door closed, missing Derek's ankle by mere inches.

"Secure the scene? What's going on? I have a right to know!" shouted Derek.

The female officer slid in behind the steering wheel. The male officer was still outside, stringing bright yellow tape from Willie's Silverado across the lawn to the front trees.

"Mr. Windward. I'm Officer Patty Ellsworth. And no, you do not have a right to know; you would like to know. And as of now, this is a homicide investigation." Officer

Ellsworth backed out and pulled away to head for Cedar Rapids Police Department.

Derek's eyes widened. He had no words.

His friend is dead? How is that even possible? And why was he being taken in for questioning? Do they think he had something to do with the death of his friend Willie?

Suddenly, his shoulders drooped. His chin trembled, and his eyes filled with tears. Willie was gone. Gone forever.

"Mr. Windward. How long have you known Mr. Ashbluff?" asked Ellsworth.

It didn't take long to reach the station. She pulled in and parked the cruiser in the spot directly across from the front door.

For a brief moment, they sat in the dark. Derek could not speak. A single tear made its way down his flushed cheek.

"I am sorry for the loss of your friend," said Ellsworth in a soft voice. "It's not only a shock, but..." She didn't bother to finish.

Derek leaned forward and placed his head in his trembling hands. He didn't care if she saw him cry. His best friend was gone.

Patty could hear Derek weeping. She reluctantly opened the cruiser door. Derek's night had just begun. She knew it would be extremely hard to question him in his emotional state. But it wasn't up to her. The detectives would be coming back to interview Derek.

Patty motioned for him to exit the vehicle. Derek sniffed and wiped his nose with the back of his hand.

"I'll take you home when you're finished, Mr. Windward," said Patty. "Let's get this over with."

Derek went inside the police station. Minutes later, he was seated alone in a small, windowless room with a round table and two folding chairs.

Suddenly, he felt drained. Willie had no family, or none he ever spoke of. It would be up to him to arrange his friend's funeral. But he knew there would be an autopsy performed, since Willie's death was considered a homicide. The thought of slicing open a body and removing its organs was disgusting.

The door to the interview room opened. It was the two detectives from the homicide scene. One stood against the wall, while the other sat down.

"Mr. Winward, I'm Detective Adrian Wixx, and this is Detective Jack Yarrow. We just have a few questions, and you'll be on your way. Officer Ellsworth will drive you home when we're finished." Wixx opened his folder and pulled out a pen from inside his suit coat. "How long have you known Mr. Willie Ashbluff?" he asked.

Derek's mind drifted back to the first time he met Willie. It seemed like just yesterday.

"Since I moved into my house next door. Roughly about ten years or so. We hit it off immediately. He was... different." Derek lowered his head as his eyes filled once again with tears.

"I know this is difficult for you, Mr. Winward," said Det. Yarrow. "We'd like to bring Mr. Ashbluff's killer to justice."

Derek gave a slight nod. "How did he die?" he asked Derek.

Both men looked at one another.

"We can't tell you until we receive the official cause of death from the medical examiner. But it's safe to say it was indeed a homicide," said Det. Wixx.

"I don't know how I can help...I told the dispatcher everything I know, which isn't really much at all," said Derek.

"You seem really upset. The two of you must have been close. Talked about things only buddies would talk about. Did Mr. Ashbluff ever tell you he was having trouble with a certain person? Do you know of anyone who would have wanted to cause Mr. Ashbluff harm?" asked Det. Wixx.

Derek remained silent for a moment. He searched his mind for any kind of clue that could help the police catch this madman. "As far as I know, Willie didn't have too many friends."

"What did you mean before when you said Mr. Ashbluff was different?" Det. Yarrow shifted on his feet. He crossed his thick arms.

"Different in the sense of being a loner, I guess. He kept to himself. His appearance was kind of rough. Long gray hair pulled back into a ponytail. A scraggly beard. Old, worn clothes. He...he looked like a homeless person. But Willie...he never bothered anyone. Didn't like to be around people. I invited him several times to go grab a beer at Barney's Pub. He said he was claustrophobic and hated crowds. So, we'd buy a six pack and sit around in our back yards and shoot the shit." Derek's head once again dropped.

"What about family?" asked Det. Wixx. "Did he talk about his family?"

Derek shook his head back and forth. "Willie didn't have family...or at least that's what he told me. I never saw anyone visit him. He never talked about it. I didn't push the subject. I figured he'd tell me if he wanted me to know," explained Derek.

"Married? Divorced? Girlfriends? Boyfriends? Romantic interests?" pushed Det. Wixx.

"None of them. He'd go to work and come home. He enjoyed yard work. Watched a lot of movies. At least once a week, we'd have movie night. Order pizza, drink beer, and pick out an old movie to watch. He liked comedies," said Derek.

"What kind of job did Mr. Ashbluff do?" Derek was growing more and more tired. The questions seemed to be irrelevant to solving the homicide.

"Willie worked on the railroad. He walked the track, inspecting the rails. I thought it was a boring job. But Willie...he loved it. It made him feel important. He was good at it. In fact, I used to tease him about being a hobo from one of the old movies we watched together." Derek gave a half-smile at the fond memory.

"It would seem you two were close. Why did you wait almost six days before calling the police?" pushed Det. Yarrow.

Derek hesitated before he answered. "Willie is a private person. Sometimes he'd get into...a mood. Didn't want company. I thought...I thought it was one of those times. I'd give him space. But I knew there was something off when his lawn wasn't cut and his bushes weren't trimmed. He was a stickler about his yard. We have a thing on our street--Mentone...the lawns are mowed on Wednesdays. It's just something we do."

The two detectives remained quiet.

"It started about five years ago. A bet. Anyone who didn't have their lawns mowed on Wednesdays had to buy a six pack for those who did. It caught on. And once everyone kept their lawns mowed on a Wednesday...well, it stuck." Derek shrugged his shoulders.

"How about a grudge against him? Maybe in the neighborhood?" asked Wixx.

Derek shook his head. "No. No. No one I know of... like I said before...Willie wasn't everyone's cup of tea, but to go to the extent of murdering him? I just don't understand," said Derek, with sad eyes.

"Mr. Winward, I think that's all the questions we have for the moment. We'll keep in touch if we have any more," said Wixx. "Officer Ellsworth will take you home."

And with that said, the two detectives left Derek alone. Seconds later, Officer Ellsworth opened the door.

"Mr. Winward...I'll take you home now." She gestured toward the door.

Derek slowly stood up and walked out with the police officer.

Derek hardly slept a wink. He tossed and turned until he could stand it no more and got up. It was still dark outside. The clock read 3 a.m. He glanced out at Willie's house. The yellow tape surrounding Willie's home fluttered in the wind. His stomach clenched in knots.

Was he home when Willie was murdered? Why didn't he hear anything?

The coffee was bitter-tasting. Derek added more half-and-half. It didn't matter. His stomach still flipped and flopped. His eyes burned from lack of sleep. He already knew he wouldn't be going into work. A slight headache began to crawl up the base of his skull. Derek plopped down on his newly purchased sofa. The cushions were hard and uncomfortable. Why did he buy it? As he closed his eyes, his mind drifted to the last time he and Willie had shared a beer together.

Before he knew it, he'd fallen asleep. The nightmare was vivid. Flashes of red. A huge butcher knife with serrated edges on both sides. A piercing pain. A scream. And then darkness.

A loud knock awoke him from the void.

Derek jerked to the abruptness from the continuous noise. His throat felt dry. It was light outside. The sun was shining. The knock came again. He staggered to get to his feet. A dull headache still lingered.

"Hold on!" he shouted.

Derek opened his front door. A tall man in a black tailored suit smiled. His gray hair had been meticulously cropped close to his head, and his beard was groomed by a barber. But it was the face that gave Derek pause.

"Good morning, sir. I'm Billie Ashbluff—Willie's twin brother," said the strange man.

Derek couldn't comprehend. *Was he still asleep and this was a dream?*

"The Cedar Rapids Police gave me my brother's address. And they told me you were the one who called my brother in as a missing person. I know it's early, but may I come in and talk with you about my brother?" he asked.

Derek still didn't move. His mind couldn't wrap around the fact that Willie had a twin.

"Yeah...sure...come on in."

Derek unlocked the screen door and let Willie's twin inside. Billie Ashbluff inched his way and stood to the side.

"I'm sorry...where are my manners...let's sit by the table. Can I get you coffee or tea?" asked Derek. His mouth felt like sandpaper.

"No. Thank you." Billie pulled out a chair. "I was also told you were a good friend to my brother. He talked

14

about you often when I called. I'm assuming it was you, since he never gave me a name." Billie Ashbluff folded his hands on top of the cluttered table.

"I can't get over...how much you look like him. I mean...I know you're a twin, but then again you don't. You look completely opposite. And as long as I've known Willie, he never mentioned he had a twin," said Derek.

Billie Ashbluff gave a half-smile. "Willie was a private man. He kept things like that to himself. Willie didn't like to share." Derek stared at the man. He couldn't get over how different yet identical the two men were.

"I wanted to...I wanted to thank you for caring so much about my brother. Calling the police was the best thing to do. I haven't learned much about his death because it's an open investigation. I'm assuming once the police obtain the medical examiner's report, we'll know more. But again, thank you."

Billie extended his hand. Derek grasped it. It was soft and warm.

"Well, I should be on my way. I'll be arranging the funeral services once his body is released." Billie stood up to leave.

"Thanks for stopping by. Please let me know if you hear anything else from the police," said Derek.

"Of course...of course. I will indeed give you a call. I have to be on my way."

Billie Ashbluff opened the front door and left. Derek slowly closed it.

"A twin...huh...who would have known?" said Derek to himself.

Attendance at the Westford Funeral Home was light. A prayer group from the Cedar Rapids Lutheran church donated a large floral arrangement. Several people from the town came by and paid their respects—or maybe just to curb their curiosity.

It had been an open casket. Willie Ashbluff looked like he was sleeping. Derek still couldn't believe his friend was dead. And he still didn't know how he died. No one had contacted him to let him know. But why should they? He wasn't family. Maybe Billie knew the details.

Derek glanced about the funeral parlor. A few people sat in the chairs, conversing with one another. The funeral director stood near the door. But Billie was nowhere to be seen.

"Hello...my name is Derek Winward. I was a good friend and neighbor of Willie," he said to the tall, elderly gentlemen dressed in a black suit.

The older man turned to face Derek and held out his hand. "I'm deeply sorry for your loss, Mr. Winward. I'm Alex Stafford, the funeral director here at Westford Funeral Home." Both men shook hands.

"I was wondering if maybe you've seen Billie Ashbluff around. I would like to speak with him," said Derek.

Alex Stafford's eyebrows crunched. He remained silent for a brief moment. "I'm sorry. I don't know a Billie Ashbluff. Is he a relative of Mr. Willie Ashbluff?"

Derek shoved his hands in the pockets of his dress slacks. "Wait...I thought Billie Ashbluff handled the funeral arrangements for his twin brother Willie?" Derek frowned.

"No, Mr. Winward. Funeral arrangements were handled by Mr. Will Ashbluff many years ago, when he was alive and well. As for a Mr. Billie Ashbluff, he may exist, but I have no knowledge of him," said Stafford.

Just then, Stafford immediately turned his attention to those entering the viewing area.

Derek stepped to the side. He scratched his jaw. *Was he dreaming when he met Billie Ashbluff? Impossible!*

Derek remained at the funeral parlor until it emptied. He stood alone, looking down at his friend. His eyes gleamed with tears.

"You were very fond of my brother, were you not?" asked a voice from behind.

Derek jerked his head back and swirled about.

"Billie?" said Derek. The strange man was dressed exactly the same as when Derek had met him a few days before. "You're...you're here." Derek stepped back.

"And why wouldn't I be?" asked the man who called himself Billie Ashbluff.

"I asked Alex Stafford, the funeral director, if he saw you...he said he didn't even know who you were. You told me you were going to handle Willie's affairs. Stafford told me Willie handled all this years ago. So...who are you really, and what do you want with me?" questioned Derek.

The mysterious man smiled. "I'm here to help you solve the murder."

Derek forced a half-grin. "Me? You're mistaken. The police are investigating Willie's murder. You should go talk to them if you have any information." He turned back to face the casket.

"They're looking in the wrong direction. They're looking at it as a crime of convenience. And it's not!" said the man called Billie.

Derek let out a sigh. "Look...whoever you are...I'm not a cop. Okay? Go tell the detectives handling the case."

"I told you. They're looking at this crime the wrong way. I can help you solve my brother's murder!" exclaimed the man.

"Why me? Why can't you solve it yourself? You say you're his brother...what do you need me for?" asked Derek. He narrowed his eyes.

"I...can't," whispered Billie.

"And why not?" persisted Derek. He took a step forward.

"Because...like my brother...I'm dead," muttered Billie. Derek scratched his jaw. "I know this is hard to believe, but it's true."

"I'm not sure what's going on here...but today is not the day. I'm grieving a good friend of mine." Derek turned to face the open casket once more.

"Mr. Winward, the funeral parlor will be closing shortly. Please pay your final respects, so we may prepare for the burial tomorrow," said Stafford.

Derek swirled around. The older gent was leaving the room. Derek stood alone. Billie was nowhere to be found.

"Billie," called out Derek.

"Do you believe me now?" asked Billie. Derek jumped, startled by the close proximity of the voice behind him.

"What the...how did you..." stuttered Derek.

"I tried to tell you, Derek, I am not of this world. You could say I'm in-between because my work here isn't finished," said Billie.

Derek rubbed his eyes. They burned from tears and the lack of sleep.

"If that's true, where's Willie?" asked Derek.

"My brother moved on. His death was underserving, but he had no need to stay. You could say he went on to a better place," said Billie.

"Why am I the only one who can see you?" questioned Derek.

Billie shrugged his shoulders. "I'm not sure how this spirit stuff works. You were a true friend to my brother. You had a connection. Maybe that's why you can see me. It doesn't matter. What matters is that I know who murdered my brother, and you're going to bring this man to justice."

"Mr. Winward...please, we'd like to lock the doors. Can you please exit the building?" asked Stafford.

Derek turned on his heel to face the funeral director.

"I'm sorry, Mr. Stafford. I'm leaving now."

Derek quickly walked past the man and exited into the empty parking lot. It was dark and damp outside. The night air turned cold. He started his car and made his way home.

As he pulled into his driveway, he noticed the yellow crime scene tape had been removed from Willie's house. It sat dark and silent. Once again, tears swelled within his grainy eyes. His thoughts went instantly to the pact they'd both made with the neighbors—lawns mowed on Wednesdays on Mentone Avenue. He chuckled to himself. Willie got a kick out of it. He never missed a Wednesday. Now, there would be no more mowing on Wednesdays for Willie. There would be no more anything for Willie.

The following day, Willie Ashbluff was buried in Heaven's Gate Cemetery, which sat on the outskirts of Cedar Rapids. It was brisk, and the wind was blustery. The funeral director read a few lines from his book as the casket was lowered into the cold ground.

Derek said goodbye to his good friend, Willie. His life would change drastically without his buddy. He didn't bother going back to the funeral parlor for a light lunch. Instead, he drove home to sulk.

Once inside his warm car, he turned on the radio. News of the murder filled his vehicle. The police were actively working on the murder investigation. They gave a number for the tip line for anyone who knew or saw anything the day of the murder.

"I told you they haven't a clue," said the voice from the back seat.

Derek stomped on the brakes. A horn blared. He glanced in his rearview mirror. Billie sat in the middle of his back seat.

"Look buddy, I don't know who you are or what you are, except you pop up at the most inconvenient time and strangest places," said Derek in a firm voice.

Another blare of a horn.

"Alright...alright, I'm going," muttered Derek as he pressed down on the gas pedal.

Once again, he headed straight for home, only to glance back to see he was once again alone.

"I'm going crazy," he whispered.

Several minutes later, he pulled into his garage. Once inside his house, he grabbed the whiskey bottle from the shelf, then poured himself a stiff one.

The brown liquid burned his throat as it smoothly slid down. He hated funerals—especially when it was someone he cared about. Plopping down on the worn sofa, he leaned his head back and closed his eyes. Within minutes, he was fast asleep.

The visions were vivid. A strange man was behind Willie's house. It looked as if he was jimmying the screen door open. Derek watched as if it were a movie trailer. Seconds later, the man entered Willie's home. But Derek could do nothing. His feet were frozen in the spot where he stood. Then the strange man dashed from the back of the house to the front. Along the way, he stopped and looked directly at Derek, who was peeking from his window. The man instantly became familiar. In fact, the man smiled and waved at Derek. It was their neighbor from a few doors down, Barney Whipple. Derek couldn't believe his eyes. His baggy shirt and pants were soaked in red. Again he waved, then disappeared.

Derek awoke with a start. Sweat lined his brow. His mouth was dry. He staggered to get up. The bottle of whiskey fell to the floor, staining his carpet.

"Damn," said Derek under his breath.

"I told you it wasn't a crime of convenience. You *do* know my brother's killer. You just needed a little help to remember," said Billie. The mysterious entity was sitting in Derek's old recliner.

"How did you get inside my house? My door is locked, and so are my windows," said Derek.

Billie stood up and stretched. "If you think locking your doors will keep me out...well, you still don't believe me. I'm here to help you solve my brother's murder. As soon as I know the police have got that...that killer in jail, I can be on my way."

Derek rubbed his grainy eyes. He glanced at the empty chair. The sun was peeking out behind the white clouds. It was early morning. Derek's dream had felt so real. What he couldn't understand was, why would Barney Whipple kill Willie? It didn't make sense. But if there was a chance his dream was actually true, he would find out before calling the police.

Derek watched as Barney Whipple exited his home and got into his beat-up Chevy truck. It was Wednesday, and all the lawns on Mentone Avenue would be cut—including his. Derek hired the teenager down the street to cut his lawn. Even though it was still cold outside, the grass seemed to keep growing.

Whipple backed out of his driveway and never glanced at the car sitting a few houses down, parked on the street. Derek had ducked down just in case the old man looked his way. Minutes later, he was following Whipple into the city, until finally he pulled into the lot next to a pawnshop. Derek patiently waited until Whipple was buzzed inside. Putting on sunglasses and a baseball cap, he strolled to the locked door and pressed the doorbell. Instantly, it buzzed, and he went inside.

It was a typical pawnshop, with display cases full of coins, jewelry, and collectibles. Whipple was busy with a middle-aged woman. Derek was hoping Whipple's eyesight had deteriorated enough with age not to recognize his neighbor from Mentone Avenue.

"May I help you, sir?" asked the young man behind the counter.

Derek glanced up at him and forced a half-smile.

"I need a present for my wife. It's our anniversary," lied Derek.

The man behind the counter nodded.

"We're having a special on jewelry—forty percent off," said the clerk.

Derek walked up to where the man was standing. Whipple stood conversing with the woman just a few feet away.

"How much would you give me for the silver coins?" asked Whipple.

The woman put on a white glove and picked up one of the silver coins. She used a magnifier to examine it. "Well, this is a very nice collection of the Walking Libertys, sir. May I ask how you came about such an extraordinary collection of mint condition coins?" she asked.

21

Whipple licked his aged, cracked lips, then shifted on his feet.

"I...I had them put away in a closet. Yup, that's it. In a closet. Need some cash, so I decided to see what all I can get for them," replied Whipple, clearing his throat.

Derek looked at the collection of coins. He knew instantly the coins belonged to Willie. Those coins were his pride and joy. Many times, he'd pull them out to show Derek, telling him the story behind them.

"For the entire set, I can offer you five thousand dollars cash. Do you accept the offer?" asked the woman.

Whipple scratched his head. "Five thousand, you say...in cash? Well, alright then. Where do I sign?" asked the old, murderous coot.

Derek couldn't believe it! Barney was supposed to be Willie's drinking buddy. How many times had he listened to Willie talk about Barney and how they'd been good buddies for years? Yet there Barney stood, selling Willie's prized possession, without an ounce of guilt. Willie was murdered for a bunch of coins?

Derek knew *now* what he had to do. Without hesitation, he contacted the detectives handling Willie's murder. They were more than interested in such a promising lead, especially since Derek was a witness to the actual sale of Willie's possessions.

Derek scrolled through the news feed on his phone. A headline jumped out: MAN ARRESTED IN THE MURDER OF WILLIE ASHBLUFF. He let out a sad sigh.

"Well, you should be proud of yourself. My brother will have justice after all," said a familiar voice. "And as for me, I will no longer grace you with my presence. My time here has finally come to an end," said Billie, his body fading in and out.

Derek gave a slight wave. "If you happen to see Willie, tell him...tell him...I miss my friend and I'll never forget him."

Without saying another word, Billie's wobbly image disappeared once and for all.

Night in the City
By Brian Quinn

Where the Monsters Are
By Mike Morgan

Malcolm Tensor was a spy for the British government--one of the best. Sixteen years after wild magic was unleashed on an unsuspecting world and monsters stalk every corner of the globe, he's the leader of a Kill-or-Contain squad. His mission: to scour the north of the UK for unregistered magical creatures and... take care of them by whatever means necessary. He, too, was transformed by the explosion of magic so long ago, but he's still a patriot, and he knows his duty. When terrorists strike at the heart of the new order, Tensor is astonished to find his team reassigned to normal duties. Why is he being sidelined? Why does the government need so many monsters rounded up? Tensor won't stop until he finds the answers, no matter the cost. There is evil lurking beneath the center of London... evil older than anything he can imagine...

https://www.hiraethsffh.com/product-page/where-the-monsters-are-by-mike-morgan

Inverted Centers
Tyree Campbell

The apartment manager who opened the door looked the part in his rather white T-shirt and dark, food-stained trousers. He needed a shave and forty fewer pounds, and he looked very tired. But he was sober, and he had bathed this week.

I identified myself as Adrianna Holton, Oliver Holton's granddaughter. The name that appears on my legitimate driver's license is Carmen Black. Age 28, brown, black, five-ten, 144 go with that, not always with accuracy.

"Leo Bastianini," said the manager, and stuck out a beefy hand. He had no accent. Third generation at least, I guessed, and breathed a sigh of relief—my Italian was very rusty.

"I tried the door," I told him. "There was no answer. I was wondering, can you let me in so that I can wait for him? It's kind of a surprise. He hasn't seen me in five years."

"Granddaughter?" Bastianini repeated, blinking in the harsh light of the hallway. "*Nipotina?*"

I dimpled what I hoped was a winning smile. "If it wouldn't be any trouble," I said apologetically. "I'm sure he'll be back soon, and he'll be so excited . . ."

"Sure, sure. No problem." Bastianini reached inside his apartment and took a ring of two keys from the wall, and handed them to me. "Just make sure I get them back, a'right?" he added, and closed the door on my expressions of gratitude.

I *wasn't* sure Holton would be back soon, of course. He'd been missing for four days, and I'd been hired by his daughter to find him.

The wooden steps in the staircase creaked as I climbed to the second floor, and grit crackled under my boots as I negotiated a path down the litter-strewn hallway to Number 15. The key worked with some difficulty. The cold steel of the U.S. Army .45 automatic stuck under the waistband of my jeans and concealed under my jersey was a comfort as I stepped inside and closed the door before anyone emerged into the hallway to check on the source of my echoes. No one protested my entry, so I looked around.

Holton's taste in furniture, like mine, ran to early Goodwill. In the living room he had a couch and a stuffed chair that did not match, and a maple veneer coffee table and a green and gray throw rug. The walls, antique brown, were completely bare. An opening in the far right corner led to the kitchenette, which contained nothing remarkable. The door in the far left corner opened into the bedroom, in which I found an unmade twin bed, a dresser with the bottom drawer missing, and a nightstand with a lamp atop it. One of the casters on the bed had been replaced by a block of wood. The lamp lacked a bulb.

Olivia Stamford, Holton's daughter, had described her father to me as a tinkerer, an inventor. She'd said this with distaste, as if merely by uttering the words, grease and oil and electrical discharges might blacken her expensive tweed suit and white silk blouse. Given such finery, the glasses and the dishwater hair seemed out of place—surely she could afford contacts and an appointment with a competent stylist—but, having supposed initially that I was the receptionist, she received no sympathy from me. Accustomed as I was to the sartorial excesses of Wal-Mart, I added a zero to my usual fee—she could damn well afford that.

The couch and chair yielded forty seven cents and a dime, respectively. A matchbook that hawked the atmosphere at *Al's Red Dog*, from the drawer in the nightstand, gave me somewhere else to go. I had rather hoped for more: dirty dishes, old pizza boxes, a discarded sock—something tangible to support Bastianini's and Stamford's assurances that Holton was the tenant. *Someone* had slept here; the rumpled bed was proof of that. But it didn't have to be Holton.

Given what Stamford had told me about Holton's work and interests, I might reasonably have expected to

27

find some tools, equipment, perhaps even an invention or two. But there was nothing to suggest that Holton was mechanically inclined.

I returned the key to Bastianini with a promise to return later. Before leaving I peeked into the apartment mailbox and found only a bill and an advertisement addressed to Occupant. I folded them and stuffed them into my back pocket; I could use the coupons.

*   *   *

On the way back to the office—I drive an unobtrusive beige Mazda, if it matters—I conducted a mental summary. Oliver Holton owned a smart phone but so far did not respond to messages, and he lived in an apartment. The cell number might have been anyone's. The apartment was thought to be Holton's, but anyone might have slept there. The old man was retired, which meant he had no one to report to. His pension from Plancher Industries went into direct deposit, so his bank hardly ever saw him. He owned a small white pickup, not parked in the apartment lot, but I was not about to go scouring The City for small white pickups.

That left *Al's Red Dog*. I raised Lydia on my smart phone, set it on the passenger seat while I drove, and heard the customary, "The City Police, Third Precinct, Davenport."

I said, "As if you didn't have caller ID, Officer Davenport."

"Response procedure," said Lydia. "I'm a little busy."

"Making coffee, or filing reports?"

"That's not funny," she snapped, which meant one of those was accurate. Then, softer: "'Sup, Honk?"

"*Al's Red Dog*."

"Meet you there after I get off. Say, five?"

"Lydia," I sighed. Eventually I was going to have to ask her to stop hitting on me, but that point hadn't arrived. Yet.

"Sorry. What about it?" she asked.

"Exactly."

"Oh." She went into helpful-yet-cautious police officer mode. "If you're going there by yourself, expect to

28

be bored rigid. Mostly it's frequented by old farts with nothing else to do but wait for God. Retirees, pensioners, that lot. We get about five calls a month to it. Last month it was one disorderly, one disturbance, and three drunks sleeping in the alley outside the back door. The first two didn't even merit charges; the last three were piled into cabs, courtesy of The City. That do it for you?"

"Thanks, Toad." I'd bestowed that on her when we were ten, and it stuck, even though she had the wart burned off her left big toe a couple weeks later. In return she'd given me Honk, in honor of the way I blew my nose during hay fever season. "What time do they open?" I asked her.

A pause. "I don't think they close," she said. "Gotta go, Honk," she added, and rang off.

I hadn't asked her for the address, but I found it on the matchbook, right above the words "always open."

*   *   *

Back at the office, I revisited the Internet data on Holton on the off-chance I might have missed something, or might need to reinterpret the data now that I'd seen his apartment. Failing that, I glanced at Holton's mail, on the desk where I'd tossed it. The advert did have coupons, but I'm not into yogurt. The bill was for a six-month renewal of a self-storage unit on the west side of The City. Three hundred dollars was due at the end of this month; Holton had two weeks left in which to pay it. I gave *Help Yourself Storage* a call.

A male voice answered, gruff yet polite. "Aitch Why Ess."

After I gave my real name and identified myself as Holton's granddaughter, I asked if I could pay for his unit, he being out of the country for the next month. When he hesitated, I added, "Will cash be okay?"

"Yeah, cash, sure," he replied, and this time there was no hesitation at all.

I rang off, now clear on the sort of operation at HYS. Payments by plastic or check left a paper trail. Cash left no trace, which meant the manager could pocket the

29

money as if it had come to him under the table. It also gave me a bit of leverage, if I needed it.

I raided the utility box for a crowbar and a new lock, and stopped along the way at the bank to deposit Stamford's check and to get the necessary cash. Afternoon traffic was light, but still it took me a full half-hour to reach the storage facility. Like many such places, it was located in a flood plain. After parking in front of the office, I made sure the jersey hem was pulled down and taut—I don't have all that much to show, but it was now clear I wore nothing underneath—and entered.

Aronson, the manager, proved to be around Holton's age, which was sixty-eight. He looked clean and fit enough, and his desk was more organized than mine. Seeing me, he slipped off his International Harvester baseball cap and slicked back what remained of his graying hair, and made his way around the desk to the service counter.

"Ms Black?" he asked, and I nodded, although he was not looking at my head. His eyes, however, went to the twenties in my hand, and silently counted them with me to fifteen. He scooped them up and tucked them somewhere under the counter.

"I don't need a receipt," I told him, "as long as this transaction doesn't come back to me."

"No problemo, no problem," he said.

"But I would like to see the unit," I went on. "And Grampa didn't tell me the number or give me a key." I laughed, and added, "He was so excited about visiting Cancun. I even had to pay his electric, gas, and water."

Aronson opened a register and reversed it so that it was right-side up to me. "Gotta sign in and out," he told me. "Regulations."

I did so.

"It's number two-oh-seven. Second row down. You say you don't have a key?"

I gave him my best pitiful look, still making sure that my jersey was taut. "He forgets things sometimes, when he's excited," I said, and gave him a crooked grin. "He's not like you. This is a neat office, and I bet you know where everything is."

"You bet. Just a sec, I'll get the key."

Which made the crowbar and the new lock unnecessary. While he got it, I checked the register to see when Holton had last visited the unit. I did not expect to find it as recent as three days ago. And he hadn't signed out.

"Here you go, Ms Black," said Aronson, handing me the key. "Don't forget to stop by on your way out."

"I'll do that, of course, Mr. Aronson," I said.

I could feel his eyes still on me as I headed for the door, so I walked by placing one foot in front of the other, to make my body sway more. A lot of what I do is misdirection. Cash and boobs had made him abandon his security practices. Olivia Stamford's chances of getting that key stood somewhere between slim and zero.

As HYS did not provide locks for the units, Holton almost certainly had to purchase his. Given the well-worn condition of the key, he came here often—often enough to make his apartment redundant. I did the lock, raised the door . . . and found what looked like a workshop. Pliers and hammers and drills, oh, my! A set of tools for microcircuitry. Well, that figured, sort of. Holton had retired from Plancher Industries as a Senior Engineer; undoubtedly he wanted to keep his hand in. But into what?

I looked around. Nothing appeared to have been assembled. All I saw was a motley of tools, some particle board, and various lengths of metal that might have supported a framework, all around the perimeter of the interior. The middle of the floor was clean: not a scrap of sawdust or shaved metal to be seen. I could only conclude that he had been building something, and had completed it. And perhaps was now out gallivanting about in it. Or with it. Or had sold it.

I locked the door, and returned to the office to sign out on the register. Aronson still had lowered eyes, and watched while I signed. Quickly I scanned the other entries and found Holton's again. He hadn't signed out.

When I pointed this out to Aronson, he said, "Yeah, that happens. Sometimes they forget."

"I'll stop by again sometime," I told him, and once more felt his eyes on me as I walked out the door.

I was about ten minutes from the office when I realized the light blue sedan, might've been a Nissan, had made the same turns I'd made. It stayed four or five vehicles behind me. I did not recall having acquired the tail, or having seen it at HYS. But then, I hadn't expected to be followed. This was a minor missing-persons case, and as far as I knew only two people were aware that I was pursuing it.

The Nissan drove past after I turned into the parking lot I shared with the other small businesses in the strip mall. There was no point in hiding; obviously they knew who I was and what I did for a (modest) living, including this case. But the surveillance served to caution me that this might be more than a simple case of a missing old man.

Accordingly, I looked a little deeper into Olivia Stamford's background. I already knew that her parents were related to the Connecticut Stamfords—another reason to add a zero to my fee—and that she had graduated from UConn with a business degree. Earlier I'd noticed her occupation as "independent contractor," but I'd assumed that to be a fancy way of saying that she hired out to corporations for specific assignments. Her record included stints at places listed in *Fortune 500*. Whatever she did, she was good at it.

A little horned guy in the back of my head pointed out that "independent contractor" might be a euphemism for Mafia button man. Not that anyone in *Fortune 500* would balk at a temporary business association with one of the Families, but I couldn't see how that could be related to Oliver Holton. It might, however, be related to Plancher Industries.

A few phrases from Buzzkill's "I Want Your Flesh" alerted me to an incoming call and reminded me that I needed to download another ring tone, as I did not want that one to go off while I was with a client. I could barely make out Toad's voice, what with the noise in the background. She said, "On my way. Meet you there." She rang off before I could tell her to amp down The Clash.

*　　*　　*

The light blue Nissan was nowhere to be seen as I drove out to *Al's Red Dog*, but that didn't mean the surveillance hadn't changed vehicles. I kept a watchful eye out, and made a couple of turns that should have detached a tail from the rest of the pack, but all that accomplished was to tie myself up in traffic. Side roads without left-turn lanes should be demolished.

Toad is never difficult to find, once you know her general location. In this case, she'd appropriated a barstool and was sipping an umbrella-shaded concoction from a glass the size of a pitcher, but it's the vermilion hair that gets attention. That and the five-five one-ten body she hangs her freckled flesh on. In the office she'd worn a pastel green pants suit, and had seen no reason to change on my account. Demure she was, but she had the several old men who'd already arrived wishing they were three decades younger.

Not that a pick-up would've been successful. Toad was tilted every which way, but she was also *ad hoc* monogamous, and she was there to meet me. Thin lips glossed with strawberry beamed a smile at me as I walked through the haze of alcohol to join her. "Took you long enough," she said, and adjusted the umbrella in order to take a big sip.

I signaled the barkeep, a gruff black man who'd received too many weak tips; old men and women tend to bestow gratuities in amounts based on their own era, back when the minimum wage was less than a dollar an hour and coins actually rang instead of clunked. His white apron was crisp and clean, and his name tag read Lowell. I got a tentative smile from him—my generation was a tad more generous. "Chivas on a rock," I told him, and he hustled off.

"I was busy checking for tails," I told Toad. "Nothing."

"You sound disappointed."

"I had one earlier today."

The tumbler arrived, and I let him keep the two-dollars change.

"But not this time," I added, to Toad, along with a "Salud!"

"Maybe you just didn't see it."

I shrugged. "Or maybe they're so smooth that they drove on past my turns, thinking they'd been made."

"Or that. What are you working on that brings you to a place like this?"

I told her. When I finished, she said, "*Wee-urd.*"

"I didn't get the impression that a crime was involved," I said, swirling my tumbler. "Now I'm starting to wonder."

"So why here?" she asked again.

I extracted a twenty and laid it on the counter, curling my hand over it. At my nod, the barkeep came over. His glance down caught a denomination corner that I uncovered. He frowned uncertainly; I smiled.

"I'll keep it simple," I said. "What can you tell me about Oliver Holton?"

The question seemed to relax him. "Goofy old duck," he replied, and I realized he had a faint English accent. "Comes in every Wednesday, like clockwork."

"Today's Wednesday," I pointed out.

"The meeting is not until six," he replied.

"Keep talking," I urged.

Lowell's eyes went to the twenty, as if he were afraid it was devaluating. "I'm not sure what you're looking for, Miss," he said, with continental politeness. "Over at the table in the far corner you'll see five men gathered. Two more usually show up; one of them is Mr. Holton. They meet here every Wednesday."

"Okay," I said. "Why?"

"They're a stamp club," he explained. "They drink and talk about stamps. Sometimes they do a little trading or selling."

"Stamps," I repeated. "Postage stamps?"

His accent grew a little stronger. "That's right, Miss. Postage stamps." He chuckled, and added, "The old duck tried to pay his bar tab with one. Red thing, it was. It didn't have those little holes for tearing them apart; this one you had to cut from the sheet." His face screwed up as he tried to recall more details. "Two cents, it was. Something about Alaska. The bloke who bought it from Russia was on it."

"Seward?" asked Toad. "Secretary of the Interior Seward?"

Lowell nodded. "That was it. He said it was worth fifty quid . . . ah, sorry about that. Dollars. Fifty dollars. I turned it down, of course," he added. "The manager likes cash, don't you know?"

"Cover my hand," I said, and he did. I drew mine from underneath his, leaving him to crumple up the twenty and stuff it into an apron pocket. I didn't see any surveillance cameras around; I hoped the manager wasn't too finicky.

"Holton's a philatelist," said Toad, after Lowell moved off to serve another patron.

I shook my head. "I had the impression he was straight."

Toad choked on her drink. "No, no," she said, swallowing to recover. "It means he collects stamps. Honk . . . another reason they didn't follow you here could be because you had already gone to the place they wanted to know about."

I thought about that. Effectively Holton had converted his storage unit into a workshop of sorts. Perhaps Olivia Stamford—it had to be her or some colleagues—regarded the unit as significant.

"Shall we join the Stamp Club?" I asked.

"Can't hurt," she replied.

She finished her drink; I took mine with. The old men made room for us at their table. I decided to stick to my cover as Adrianna Holton, as it might open a door or two with them.

"I wanted to visit my grandfather," I added. "He wasn't at his apartment. I was told he attended club meetings here."

The expected questions followed. No, I did not collect stamps, but I was interested in them. I liked the older stamps—an admission that earned me smiles from the old men; there's nothing like the presence of couple of young women to make old men pat their meager hair in place and rub their cheeks for that horrid five-o'clock shadow. I added that Grandfather had at least instilled in me a passing interest in the hobby.

All too soon the conversation reverted to the technical aspects of philately. But in any gathering there is always someone who remains on the periphery, who doesn't know how to fit in though he wants to. Fred Daly was one such. He gave us an appreciative once-over without ogling, and resumed listening, and nodding at the right times. He had the usual septuagenarian wrinkles and sparse gray hair. He might live longer if he lost ten pounds. He had lonely blue eyes—he wanted to belong, but never had. I felt sorry for him. If he were four decades younger, I'd've nudged Toad to leave.

I leaned closer to him. "I don't understand a word they're saying," I told him. "Could you translate?"

His smile did not expose his dentures. "It's about a stamp your grandfather assured us he would bring," he said. "The Mauritius one-penny orange. You don't know the story?" I shook my head, as did Toad, and he went on, relaxing and gathering enthusiasm as he spoke. "I'll give you the short version. In 1847, postage stamps were still a novel concept. The wife of the governor of Mauritius sent out invitations to a ball, and to impress her guests she wanted to use postage stamps for the envelopes, so she ordered some printed. These stamps were legal frank—that is, proper postage stamps.

"So she mailed out the invitations, and destroyed the rest of the stamps. You can imagine their scarcity now. Most all copies of the one-penny orange and two-penny blue are in museums or in the hands of private—and very wealthy—collectors. To give you an idea, there is an envelope bearing one copy of each of the two denominations—it's known as the Bordeaux—and it was last sold for four million dollars."

"Judas Priest," breathed Toad.

"It has been said that, pound for pound, a rare postage stamp is the most expensive item in the world," said Daly.

"I believe it," I said. "But what does that have to do with my grandfather?"

"Ah." Daly sat back, and took a sip of beer from his mug. "Ollie claims he owns a copy of Mauritius 1, the catalogue number—that would be the orange one. Now, he's made a few boasts before this, but he's come through on his word." He shook his head. "I simply don't see how he can produce the Mauritius. None of us are that rich."

We laughed. "Maybe it's a fake," Toad suggested.

"The others haven't been," argued Daly. "The higher value singles, like the 1893 four-dollar Columbian, were warranted as genuine by the American Philatelic Society. Each one came with a certificate. No, they weren't fake. But the Mauritius . . ." He shook his head doubtfully.

"It looks like it's going to be the five of us," the club president announced. His gaze went to Toad and me. "And two guests?" At this point, she and I got up to leave. "Shall we get started? Old business?" he finished.

I wrote my phone number on a coaster and gave it to Daly. "Would you please call me if he shows up?" I asked, and he agreed that he would.

With nothing else for Toad and me to do but drink, we got out of there. Toad made a vague offer that I declined with a head shake. We hugged, and went our separate ways.

*　　*　　*

Meditation and a good night's sleep made me rethink the case in the morning. At the office I sat down with a mug of coffee and reviewed the new developments. Holton was in, or had come into, possession of valuable postage stamps. Stamford wanted me to find him. Her attire placed her well above my station. Valuable stamps could be authenticated by the American Philatelic Society. Holton rented a self-storage unit, the lease for which had been about to expire. Holton had not shown up at the Stamp Club meeting, which was unusual. Neither was he at his apartment. Stamford had money.

I wrote these facts down on a sheet of paper. I can use a computer, but actual print helps me to think.

Next I jotted a brief series of questions. Was Stamford in fact Holton's daughter? If no, or even if so, had she come to me because she had been tasked with locating him? By whom? Why me? What was the origin of Holton's stamps—personal collection or recent purchase?

I was tempted to cross off the bit about a collection. As an engineer, Holton surely made his share of money, but I doubted it was enough to enable him to pay tens of thousands of dollars for a scrap of colored paper. Certainly Holton did not live like someone who possessed valuable stamps, or anything else. He lived like a bored retiree who was getting by.

I called Toad at work. She answered with the usual formal greeting. "Does Oliver Holton own any property under his name in The City?" I asked her.

"You can check that yourself, Honk," she reminded me, with some asperity. "All private information is available on the Internet, you know."

"All the above-board info," I agreed. "I'm looking for something down a few layers, where only hackers go."

"Any particular reason?"

"Yeah. Holton has to have money somewhere. I want to get a handle on how many zeroes. If he owns property somewhere, that could help."

"Busy tonight?"

"Toad . . . please."

Her sigh was audible over the phone. "Not what I meant. We're friends—or we used to be. Sometimes I hate eating a pizza alone."

Guilt gigged me just below the heart. "Oh, Toad. Yeah, bring one over tonight, sevenish. I'll go the sodas."

"Nothing diet."

"Never crosses my lips."

We rang off. I looked up the number for the American Philatelic Society and was about to dial it when Fred

38

Daly called. He reminded me who he was, and we exchanged pleasantries. Oliver Holton had not shown up. But . . .

"We seldom have attendees as young as you and your friend," said Daly. "Kids nowadays don't get the appeal of stamps. And why should they? Most everything postal these days is wallpaper, and not just in this country. From stamps you can learn geography, history, botany—"

"Mr. Daly."

". . . zoolo—"

"Mr. Daly."

". . . yes?"

"I'm not all that interested in stamp collecting," I told him. "I'm not Oliver Holton's granddaughter. I'm a private investigator, hired to locate him. That's all."

A silence followed, long enough to make me nervous. He hadn't hung up, but I couldn't even hear him breathing. When next he spoke, it startled me.

"I wondered whether it would come to that," he said.

I gave him the address of a nearby mom-n-pop coffee shop, and asked him to meet me there.

*   *   *

After my mug of coffee arrived, Daly showed me a newspaper clipping with a color photograph of a United States postage stamp. It was square, with a brown border and a blue center, and in the denomination of fifteen cents. It depicted the landing of Columbus. For some reason, the center had been printed upside down.

"A used copy of this stamp, properly printed, is easily affordable," said Daly. "You should be able to find one for two or three hundred dollars, depending on condition. The one you see here, with the inverted center, is an unused copy, and it was sold at Sotheby's a week ago for half a million pounds."

I masked my astonishment with a grin. "What's that in metric?"

"It depends on the rate of exchange, but I should say around six hundred fifty thousand dollars. It's *Scott's Catalogue* 119b, if you'd care to check."

I did not know what to say. "I appreciate your telling me this," I managed, and gave the coffee a try. It had cooled enough to sip. "But why are you telling me this?"

He folded the clipping and tucked it into his shirt pocket. "Because the buyer never got the stamp," he said. "Somewhere between purchase and delivery, it got lost."

I assumed it had been mailed. "What about tracking?" I asked. "Surely it was registered, and insured."

Daly shook his head. "It was to be delivered by drone courier. The stamp was packed inside; there were four witnesses and a security video to this. There were no flight interruptions or anomalies. When the drone arrived at the correct address, the packing was still inside it, but not the stamp."

"That doesn't make any sense."

"No. It doesn't. But there you are."

I asked the obvious question. "How does this concern Holton?"

Daly's face filled with wrinkles. "I don't know. But the philatelic grapevine has it that this is not the first instance of such a disappearance. I'm not the only one in the Stamp Club who thinks there's a connection, but I'm damned if I can see what it is."

"Would it have anything to do with the fact that he's missing?" I asked.

"I'm not so sure he's missing," Daly returned. "I have to wonder whether he's gone into hiding."

I dwelt on that for a few moments. You could hide in The City, but eventually the surveillance cameras, combined with facial recognition tech, would locate you— if asked to do so.

"Last night you mentioned a stamp from Mauritius," I said. "Has Holton brought any other stamps to the club?"

"Oh, yes, certainly," said Daly. He took a sip from his mug; his expression said he thought the coffee was still too hot. "Ollie even tried to pay off his bar tab with one, but finally had to try cash. Except for the four-dollar

Columbian, which Collier—he's the club president—
bought from him for eight grand, the stamps have been
in the three-figure range, sometimes less."

"But lately he's been going for bigger game," I
suggested.

"So it would seem."

I sat back, unable to think of any more questions.
Even so, I knew I had missed something. "Well . . . that's
a lot to ponder," I said at last, and got up. "Thanks for
the coffee. I'll call if I come up with anything else."

His expression darkened to glum as I left him.

*　　*　　*

Pizza arrived at my first-floor apartment in the hands
of Officer Lydia Davenport, as she announced herself.
Fourteen inches across, cut into pieces of eight.   One
hundred and fifty-three square inches of Genoa salami,
black olives, mushrooms, and extra cheese.   You'd've
thought we were still in college.

We did the usual Toad-Honk greetings, and she
stepped aside, and I started to close the door just as tires
squealed, and a pale sedan shot away from the curb in
front of the apartments.   Startled, Toad dropped the
pizza and went for the pistol in the rig behind her back.
My own weapon was in the rig slung over a chair at the
dining table.   Toad tried to risk a glance out the front
window, but I pulled her back down.

"Give it a minute," I whispered to her. I reached up
for the switch and doused the living room lights. "Maybe
they'll double back."

"Did you get a look?" she asked. "Any idea who it
was?"

I shook my head. "Where'd you park?"

"Right out front," she replied.

"Then you must have seen them."

Toad swore. "Right, right. Okay, hush, let me think."
Moments later, she spoke in a monotone. "Romeo Tango
Lima local license plate, The City code for 'rental.' Light
colored sedan. Saturn-like emblem on the trunk. Damn
headrests make it difficult to tell from behind how many

occupants." She sighed, dejected. "I got nothing else. I should call this in."

She dug out her smart phone. "No," I said. "I think it's the same vehicle that was on my tail earlier. Maybe they were just letting me know that they know I know."

"Okay. Why?"

"I don't know." I picked up the box. "Pizza's getting cold."

"That," she said, "we can do something about."

* * *

The few remaining slices in the box were cold by the time I finished bringing Toad up to date. I stuck a slice in the nuke for half a minute. It came out too hot, so I let it cool on the table. Toad had already swilled down half her soda, and declined my offer of another.

"I don't like this," said Toad. "I understand it . . . but watch yourself. This isn't just a missing-persons case." She glanced at her smart phone. "I should get going. I have an early day tomorrow."

"I thought you were on the nine-to-five shift."

"I am." She got up. "I have a spot of shopping to do, and stop at the post office for a book of stamps, and this is the only time I'll have until next week, when I start swing shift."

"Yeah," I said absently. Something she had just said had already begun to gnaw at me, but it wouldn't hold still long enough for me to stab it with a mental fork.

At the door Toad turned back around. She was wearing an expression filled with more emotions than I could count. Words to express them failed to make it to her lips. Finally she managed a, "Later," and walked outside. I watched her until she drove away.

Half an hour later I was sound asleep.

* * *

In the morning I made it to the office without surveillance, as far as I could tell. I could almost have appreciated the attention. Aside from the Holton case, I had no visitors and no prospects. After I made myself comfortable at my desk and was working on my second mug of coffee, I called the American Philatelic Society, as

I had been about to do yesterday when Daly called. On the third ring, a young-sounding woman identified herself as Adele Langley.

After we exchanged brief pleasantries, I said, "I'm trying to reach Olivia Stamford. I was told this was the number to call."

The moment of hesitation on the other end told me I had stepped on a toe or two. Whose, remained to be determined. "I'd better transfer you," said Langley, and did so before I could respond.

The next voice I heard was that of an older man, doubtless seated behind a desk and browsing the *Wall Street Journal*. He had that sort of patrician tone when he gave his name, Joseph Shapiro, and asked what he might do for me.

I gave him the same response I'd given Langley. His moment of hesitation made a lie of his answer. "I'm afraid you've reached the wrong number, Ms. Black."

When he did not elaborate, I said, "Seriously. So why was I transferred to you, then? Your switchboard receptionist certainly knew where to direct my inquiry."

"May I ask what your interest is?" said Shapiro, after another hesitation.

I told him I was a P.I. hired by Stamford.

"I see. And she gave you this number?"

The question identified the stubbed toe—I was not supposed to know who she was working for. I decided not to push the issue, made my excuses for a wrong number, and rang off.

By the time my coffee mug was empty, I found myself wishing I had Toad around, to run a few things by her. I thought about giving her a call, but she was probably still out and about. She only just had time to stop at the post office.

That mental fork stabbed about once more. I poured another mug of coffee, and walked the matter around. Stamford did not work directly for the APS, but evidently had been hired by them. Holton possessed postage stamps whose value far outpaced the finances of his station—or so it seemed. Someone had followed me around, but not to the tavern.   Several high-value postage stamps had disappeared.

It didn't add up.   I had an orange here, an apple there, some grapes nearby, next to the plum.   Calling it all fruit didn't help much.

Toad was going to the post office to buy stamps. Well, yeah, that's where you buy stamps.   If you need postage stamps, you go to the post office to buy them. You go in and you pay about twelve dollars for a book of twenty of them.

If Holton wanted a one-cent orange stamp from Mauritius, he could travel to Mauritius and buy one. With air travel and the right connections, he could do it in a day or two.   Except that Daly had said that most of the copies were in museums or in the hands of private collectors.   Either way, they probably cost a wee bit more than one cent.

Of course, if you went back to 1847, you could . . .

I snagged the car keys, squirreled into my shoulder rig, and dashed for my Dodge Caliber.   The light blue Nissan was nowhere in sight.   I pulled out and sped away, made two right turns to check for tails, and learned that I was not that interesting.   Moments later I was on my way to *Help Yourself Storage*.

Aronson was not in the office.   Although I found no signs of a struggle, I suspected he had been taken prisoner and compelled to open a certain storage unit. There was no sign of the Nissan; likely it was parked near the unit.   I stayed on foot and crept around to the next row of units, and peered around the corner.

The unit door had been raised, and the unit stood open.   At the opening stood Stamford, Aronson, and a man I did not recognize, but whose physique suggested he might be muscle.   No weapons were in evidence.   All three seemed to be waiting for something to happen, and I doubted it was my arrival.

Assuming an air of confidence I did not quite feel, I rounded the corner of the row of units and approached two-oh-seven.   As I moved, the man's right hand dipped under his suit coat.   Stamford's hand on his arms stopped him from withdrawing his sidearm. Aronson looked glum; maybe he thought I was responsible for his predicament. Well, maybe I was.

Stamford didn't seem surprised to see me. I gave her the obligatory snark of, "Fancy meeting you here," and waited for an explanation.

"You'll be paid the rest of your commission," she said. "Your work here is done. We'll handle it from this point."

I made a show of gazing into the unit. "I don't see Holton," I said. "Maybe I missed him?"

"He'll be here," said Stamford. She sounded as confident as her white pants suit with the pale blue blouse—an Italian or French signature outfit. The shoes looked like Florence leather; I wondered if they would fit me. "He had to make flight connections," she went on. "Nairobi, Rome, New York."

I grinned. "No direct flights from Port Louis to The City, then?"

"The problem with time travel," Stamford replied, "is that it's from time to time, not site to site. I'm telling you this because I think you've figured out the APS's problem. If I were you, I wouldn't pass around what you think you know. You've done well; I don't know how we missed his bill for storage rent."

"Once I found that for you, the rest was on you," I added for her. "The rules of time travel dictate that Holton has to come back here at some point. I suppose that's the equivalent of finding him. Still, I'd hate to think I fingered him for you and your, er, armed guard."

Dishwater hair washed over Stamford's shoulders as she shook her head. "No matter what you might think, Ms Black, we aren't murderers."

"Yet."

"What Holton is doing, cannot continue," she said darkly. "I feel certain we'll reach an accommodation."

Her tone was dismissive. It all but ordered me to go back to my office and wait for the check. As I opened my mouth to argue, a rush of displaced air fairly bowled me over; Stamford and Aronson and the guard as well. I might have anticipated it, had I been thinking of simple physics. By the time I recovered, Holton saw a pistol aimed at him.

I had my .45 out before the guard could turn. Evidently Holton thought that I, too, was gunning for him. He nudged a lever on what looked like a control panel. The air rang with Stamford's protest. I was closest. Had I stopped to think, I probably wouldn't have done it. I mean, nothing screams "Don't touch it!" like a mechanical device capable of transporting you to, say, a buffalo stampede where The City would eventually be.

I collided with Holton; he had slightly more meat on him than a laboratory skeleton. I also struck something that moved. I heard a whirr and a clunk. This was followed immediately by a shriek and a flash of light. Air sucked at me. I hit the concrete.

Holton towered over me, fists clenched in frustration. His red face was on the verge of tears. "Why?" he cried out. "Why?"

I managed to get back to my feet. My head swam for a moment. I looked around. "Where's the time machine?"

"Gone," wailed Holton. "It's gone, it's gone . . ."

"Mr. Holton?" said Stamford. She was holding out her hand. "I'll have the stamps back, if you please. They must be returned to their rightful owners."

Holton's thin chest puffed out. "*I* am the rightful owner," he declared. "I *bought* these stamps. I *paid money* for them."

"I'm sure you did," said Stamford, not unkindly. "But many of the stamps you bought have disappeared from private collections or from museums. You've bypassed time, Mr. Holton. The stamps had no opportunity to acquire histories. You'll have to turn them over to us; we'll determine the rightful owners. Moreover, you must also sign an agreement," here she rummaged around in her purse, "to turn over to us all schematics and designs of this machine."

"I'll get a lawyer—"

Stamford shook her head almost violently. "No lawyers. No one must know of this machine, or of what you have done." She paused, eyeing him like a shrike as she handed him the form to sign. "Well, sir?"

Holton licked his lips, and dragged a hand over his sparse gray hair. "The stamps are in a safety deposit box at The First City Bank."

"Sign," ordered Stamford.

Holton accepted a pen from her and did so. She folded the form and tucked it back into her purse. A nod dismissed the guard.

"We'll pick you up at your apartment tomorrow at nine," she announced, and followed the guard back to their car. Aronson, a non-factor in the encounter, trudged after them, a bewildered look in his eyes.

Holton's shoulders slumped. His eyes dropped to the concrete at his feet, and he shook his head slowly.

"I just wanted . . . ," he moaned. "I only wanted . . ."

I touched his shoulder. "Tell me," I urged.

"The others had such fine collections," he told me. Gradually his eyes rose to meet mine. They were filled with tears, but he was not yet crying. "They impugned my collection. I just wanted to impress them. I wanted to belong."

"To be accepted," I said.

He gave a quick nod.

"Where's your car?" I asked him.

He had to think about that. Finally he said, "I took a bus."

"I'll give you a ride back to your apartment."

He looked at me as if seeing me for the first time. "Who are you?"

I gave him my name and occupation. "Postage stamps?" I asked.

"She won't get all of them," he whispered, inviting me into a conspiracy. "I sold one for a quarter million, and I still have a couple Columbians."

"I won't tell a soul."

"No. No, I don't think you would. You have that look."

I didn't have to ask what he meant. I'd been there, trying—and failing—to impress others. Finally I had

47

learned it wasn't worth it—a lesson Holton had learned late in life. I had of course lied to him: I would discuss the outcome of the case with Toad. But she has kept my secrets over the years, and would keep this one.

"Postage stamps?" I said again, as we began walking toward my car. "That's why you traveled back in time?"

"You sound disappointed, young lady."

"No, I understand it," I protested. "It's just that, hell, you could have gone anywhere—well, any*when*. You might have watched Da Vinci paint, or waited outside the tomb to see if Jesus really came back, or witnessed the signing of the Declaration of Independence. You might have visited Roswell in 1947. Or watched Morgan hide his treasure. Oliver, you might have done so many things."

He gave me a wink and a grin. "Maybe next time, I will."

The Supervisor
Christian Riley

Two hours ago, I crept up behind my supervisor, drew my forty-five caliber handgun to the back of his head, and blew his last remaining thought into a scrambled heap upon his desk.

I have never so much as killed anything larger than a fish, and would like to say that I am not a madman, but at this point I'm not too sure anymore. The authorities will definitely think so. They will find me soon on this stormy Christmas Eve, sitting here in this restaurant eating Kung Pao Chicken, and then haul me away like an animal, where I will ultimately be thrown into some remote asylum you or I have never heard of.

Hard to blame them, really. One just doesn't walk into their place of employment and murder their supervisor, then receive a light sentence for "temporarily losing his mind". Not in this day and age. My life is over, this I know, but as God is my witness, I would have it no other way. Because in truth, the actual crime here was how I let that horrendous monster, my supervisor, take from me what any man would ever live for.

The seeds of my guilt were planted several months ago, during the affectionate unfolding of summer's tide. Teddy White transferred to our backwater town of Issaquah, Washington, from our company's headquarters near downtown Seattle. He was our new fearless leader in our charge through the sea of web development, and much to our dismay, seemed as proverbial to the notion of diplomacy as one would expect from a guy like him. It was, of course, no stretch of our imagination how we silently dubbed him "The Great White", as we talked amongst ourselves in our circles.

The Great White wants you to email that progress report to Advanced Cycle Systems... now!

The Great White just gave me that condescending smile in the break room... Yeah, yeah... that's the one.

Some of Ted's annoyances could have been more palatable if it was not for the fact that he was always delegating his duties to us. At what point does the act of "delegation", that icon of proficiency, gaggled over by upper management, bring with it a relevant salary? That's the question we would often ask ourselves in the break room, as we made sport of the topic. But it was during one of these comic reliefs, while Ben Jukowski was reproducing one of Ted's ridiculous demands with flawless appeal, that I caught my first glimpse of something strange about Ted...

Something *not quite right.*

I had stood up from the chair I was in, still laughing while Ben went on with his routine, and then walked out of the break room to use the toilet. Silently standing there, around the corner, was Ted. He had caught me by surprise, most definitely. In fact, I had even jumped a bit, which I noticed brought a moment of pleasure to his eyes.

"Having fun, Dan?"

That's what he said to me, a question I had no answer for. I tucked my head with embarrassment and cowed my way to the restroom, anxiety washing over me from the awkwardness of it all.

As expected, I fretted over the incident for quite some time, worried about how Ted would handle being the target of our jokes. But it was during this moment of anxiety that I discovered that "something" about Ted. I had remembered seeing a look upon him that was quite disturbing during that moment as I walked around the corner. He had quickly concealed the face with a smile before he posed his question to me, but I had glimpsed enough of his gesture to award me a haunted feeling for days to come. The only word I could think of as I tried to rationalize my observation of Ted was *sinister.*

Just as alarming was the fact that Ted never mentioned the incident to me (or any of us in the office) again. Of course, I alerted the others about how I caught Ted spying on our conversation, which had us all speculating when the man would bring the hammer down. But there was no change in his demeanor. Nothing new, for better or for worse, that came over us from our supervisor. Nothing except an occasional odd glance from Ted, which left me wondering what he was playing at.

A few weeks passed, and the office was storming ahead of schedule, days before Halloween. We were all in a chipper mood from our progress, and probably excited over the fact that Halloween fell on a Friday this year. Jennifer, our receptionist, made up a memo inviting us to wear costumes on the upcoming Friday, but the notice was hardly needed. There were about thirty of us at the Issaquah office, and except for myself, Ted, and a few others, most of the employees were quite young. They needed little encouragement to dress up, especially on the last day of the week, and due to years of their youthful influence, neither did the rest of us "old timers".

Ted was the questionable factor, though. He was the new guy, and considering his uptight persona, along with the fact that he made no attempts to socialize with any of us beyond the parameters of work, we all assumed he would come to the office on Halloween morning dressed as his normal self.

Friday arrived, bringing with it a thoughtful surprise for everyone. Ted regularly wore khaki pants and a button-down, long sleeve shirt. Contrasting this, he also wore Nike running shoes—his silent way of bragging to us all that he, somewhere in his fifties, was still a capable runner. But on Halloween day, Ted showed up in a three-piece suit, along with four dozen donuts, for the entire office. We were stunned. Adding to our considerable astonishment, he also made a point of interacting affably with us all. The man had dressed himself in a role demanding great respect, and played the perfect character to match.

His "costume" struck us as delightfully humorous in the beginning, but after a few hours, I could see the question hidden behind the eyes of my colleagues. I know this, because the same question danced in my head as well: *How can this guy suddenly turn into the exact person our office needed?* Ted went from "The Great White" to "The Man in White", literally overnight.

It chaffed us all. He was teasing us, mocking our intelligence, toying with our emotions. But the real kicker came at lunchtime. We were all tired of Ted at that point, no one wanting anything to do with his offensive charade anymore. Nonetheless, Ted made his way back to the break room to mingle. He was attempting to "get to know us", asking questions about our individual selves, and adding to our various conversations randomly. Fed up, I turned the tables on Ted and asked *him* questions about himself. Much to my surprise, the event was short-lived.

"So tell us, Ted, what are you supposed to be dressed up as, anyway?"

"Isn't it obvious, Dan?"

"No. Not really."

"Why, Dan... I'm a serial killer."

And then he left the room, as simple as that.

The ensuing silence felt as if someone had instantly plunged our entire break room into the arctic ocean, like one of those crab pots you see on TV.

"*Ohh-kaayy,*" Ben finally said, with a crazed roll of his eyes. Most of the others chuckled awkwardly, relying on humor to cut the edge Ted left us with. But certainly not me. I found the man's words haunting. It was almost as if I truly believed him, like he was confessing to us his "other life", in a demented way only he would conjure up.

I left the office that day telling myself it was all a practical joke; just Ted being Ted, serving us all a plateful of insults, followed by that last little morsel, just in case the taste in our mouths wasn't awful enough. I put the incident out of my head, trying not to think about it until the following Monday, when at last, Ted showed up wearing his normal khakis with his long-sleeve shirt, his normal running shoes, and his normal condescending attitude. The Great White was back in the tank, and sure enough, damn if we didn't regret it.

It was a sick game for the man, and he was still playing at it. With absolute disgust, this was what I realized later that day, when Ted came up to my cubicle and whispered in my ear, "So Dan, how do you like me now?"

Yes, my blood ran cold.

I avoided Ted as much as I could after that, letting the passage of time take with it the freshness of that creepy event. And much to my relief, so did Ted. He did that thing of his, pretending nothing had ever happened, going about his usual way. Everything was all back to normal, which I was thankful for, but always in the back of my mind, loomed that chilling suspicion about Ted... *What if?*

It would be right around Thanksgiving when I picked up another disturbing clue about Ted's character. I went to his office to give him a summary report for one of our clients—and I should note here, Ted always preferred two things about his office: he always kept his door open, and he kept his computer station to the opposite side of his desk, so that when he worked on it, he would have his back to the door. And that's how I found him when I rapped my knuckles on his door, sitting there with his eyes glued to the monitor, clicking his way through some photographs.

"Come in," he replied, never once turning his back to see who it was. As I approached his desk, with words on the tip of my tongue, I had suddenly noticed from the reflection off his monitor (due to the dark colors of the picture he was looking at, and the adjacent glare from the window to his left) that Ted was staring at this picture with a sort of frivolous, childlike grin upon his face. Intrigued by his apparent fascination, I asked him what he was looking at, after which he swiftly spun his chair around, bid me to sit down in a cheerful way not seen since Halloween Friday, then tilted his monitor at an angle suitable for the both of us to look at. Naturally, I was suspicious. But upon recognition of what were obvious "hunting photographs" on his monitor, I gracefully received his invitation to sit down. I had figured it couldn't hurt to at least humor the man.

Ted immediately went into a dreamy narrative over the pictures, stating facts about the various animals only a fellow hunter would comprehend, as well as other memorable events such as "the beauty of the river here", "the coldness of the morning there", things of that nature.

His recent trip, as he showed me, was of a turkey hunt in Eastern Oregon. I remember being considerably surprised when I noticed in the pictures a couple of his friends. I guess it never occurred to me that Ted had any friends, so distant he was with his life outside of work.

He prattled on over several more pictures, and I could see clearly that the man had a genuine passion for hunting. I, myself, had never gone hunting before, but would have to admit that the notion of doing so had always struck an interest in me. Because of my natural curiosity, I inquired more about his trips, and about other general aspects regarding the hunting process.

Ted was a child. He sprung open like a cracked water main, divulging to me that part of his life like I was one of those men in his photographs; like I was one of his hunting buddies, and to be quite honest, I was flattered by it all. I savored the moment, and remembered thinking that perhaps I had finally broken some ground with the man, a common denominator that would garner a different tone between us. At one point, to my great astonishment, Ted even proposed to take me out one day, to sort of "show me the hunting ropes" if you will.

But then, as Ted went on about more pictures, more trips, I suddenly noticed a photograph of him and a friend standing before what must have been a few dozen dead squirrels, spread out at their feet in that familiar, fresh-kill pose. I asked Ted what that was about, and he bragged gaily over how he and his "bud" shot more squirrels on that day than they had in the past.

"Do you eat squirrels, Ted?" I asked him.

"Well, you can, but there ain't much meat," he replied frankly.

Many people hunt for sport, killing for the sake of some trophy, or perhaps as a form of controlling animal populations in particular habitats. This I knew. It was one aspect about hunting that never appealed to me, but I knew it was common practice. The fact that his dead squirrels apparently fell into that category wasn't what struck me as alarming, but rather, how Ted went on about that day, and the general attitude he conveyed through his expressions. I then realized, in a sudden unnerving fashion, that Ted enjoyed killing things... just for the sake of killing.

... *Serial killers, for some deranged reason, take great pleasure in murdering life's little creatures.*

I had heard that once, somewhere, years ago. They were the words that always stuck with a person, summoned to the forefront of their thoughts at various times, from conversations, or perhaps by headlines of the evening's news. They were certainly the words summoned to the forefront of my thoughts then, as Ted gazed at that photograph, reminiscing as he did...

A sudden chill swept over me. Halloween Friday... Then that following Monday—*So how do you like me now, Dan?* The miserable events of those days came whistling back to me like a train barreling through a tunnel. I was both disappointed and disturbed. *No, Ted* wasn't *going to "show me the hunting ropes".* And Yes, *Ted just may be a real life killer!*

My thoughts went foggy. I wiped my hands on my pant-legs, trying to rid them of their sudden clamminess, as I felt the racing of my heartbeat echo in my ears. My neighbor Bob had panic attacks. He used to tell me all about them on Sunday morning, after church. The sweaty palms... difficulty breathing... "Like a little mini-heart attack, Dan!" he used to say. That's how I felt then, as Ted kept going on about those damn squirrels. I ended our conversation abruptly, on the premise that I had a ton of emails to get back to, and made my way out of his office with as much couth as possible.

"Anytime you wanna go shooting, Dan..." he offered again, on my way out.

My wife, Veronica, was an incredible cook. I mean, *incredible*. Not only could she make the best Mexican food you would ever taste in your life, but she also had a flare for creating those extreme-cuisine dishes—ones that would cost you a hundred dollars a plate in a fancy restaurant near downtown Seattle. I would often joke with her that if she ever opened a restaurant, she'd put half the competition in Seattle out of business.

She had learned her art from her mother, Lucille, who actually ran a restaurant in San Diego, before passing away ten years ago. Our young daughters, Josephine, and the twins Maria and Anabella, also loved Veronica's cooking, and would often help in the kitchen as much as they could, but mostly, they were in charge of keeping me and my sneaky fingers out. It was a wonderful family game we took part in almost every night. But when I got home that evening, the "dead squirrel evening", I found I had little appetite for much of anything. At the table, my thoughts kept wandering back to Ted. I tried to put my suspicions about him out of my mind, but it seemed an impossible thing to do. Not once in all my life had I entertained the idea of being so close to a murderer.

It was all my imagination. I was working myself up over nothing. I had to be. Ted was just an asshole; a bully who liked to impose his will on everyone. Everything, for that matter. I kept telling myself this, at least.

"What's wrong, hun?"

Veronica's words broke the spell I was under. I shrugged it off as nothing, just a lot on my mind from the office and all. What could I say? *Oh, sweetie... I just think Ted is a murderer, that's all.* I had never mentioned to Veronica my concerns about Ted. It was a regular habit for me to keep my work-related stress away from my family life, and the fact that I thought my supervisor might be a real-life serial killer, well... "Work-related stress", right?

Things turned even more frightfully upsetting for me about a week later. Veronica was a goddess. She had one of those metabolisms that wouldn't quit, the kind that made us "stocky" people complain. And even after all that rich food she would cook and eat, the fact that she gave birth to three children, and that she was in her mid-forties, she still looked as fit and gorgeous as she did when I first met her, fifteen years ago. Men loved to look at her, and the brave ones would often approach her, flirt with her as they did, and much to my pleasure, she would flirt back. It never bothered me, as I wasn't the jealous type. I knew I was a lucky man. I flaunted it.

This wasn't the case, however, when she came to the office one afternoon to drop off a client-folder I had left at the house. As I walked up to the front desk to meet Veronica, to my great horror, I found her, Ted, and our receptionist Jennifer, all laughing exuberantly, like college roommates at some party. Jennifer was only half-way into the merriment, obviously a little uncomfortable with the whole "chummy" thing Ted was putting out, but Veronica was blushed in the face, running her fingers through her long black hair as she laughed along to Ted's charming behavior.

I watched them in terror from behind a corner. I wasn't jealous, so much as I was dreadfully alarmed. My wife knew nothing about Ted, and he knew nothing about her, but right then and there, they were both getting to know a little bit about each other.

Fury and terror swept over me. I quickly broke into the scene, coughing uncomfortably to announce my arrival as I walked into the lobby. The subsequent moment reminded me of a trailer from one of those Hollywood blockbusters, a suspense thriller starring Harrison Ford: Jennifer slipped out of the scene, while Ted and my wife slowly turned their heads to my direction, reluctant as it seemed, to break away from the stare they were both sharing. Their eyes, giddy with laughter and underlined with huge smiles, fell upon me...

And then, everything turned red. My palms sprouted beads of sweat, the hair down my neck rose in alarm, yet my knees buckled as once again as Ted became my "pal". He began saying stupid things like, "How'd you get so lucky, Dan?" and "For the love of God, steal paradise while you're at it," referring to my wife, who, of course, was loving the attention. Perhaps the moment was all in good-nature, but I really wanted to swing an ice pick into the man's skull. He went on with other things as well, being grossly reasonable about the folder I left at home, even bringing up other projects he knew I was fretting over, telling me not to worry about this and that... My hero, Ted, here to save me from my predicaments under the captivated attention of my wife.

For quite some time afterward, Ted was my "buddy". Although he remained oppressive towards my co-workers, any concerns addressed to me were always tactfully overlooked or dismissed as uncontrolled incidents. Whatever the case, he kept a cool edge with me regarding work, then would occasionally ask when we were going to go shooting, or how the family was. His favorite was a simple, "How's Veronica, Dan?" It would've all been quite dandy and flattering if it wasn't for the fact that I now believed Ted was a psychopath, a real life murderer walking amongst us. But unfortunately, it was during the unfolding of these events where I made my first *real* mistake with the man.

***

Ted was a very shrewd person. Obviously, he was shrewder than any of us at the office gave him credit for, but nonetheless, Ted was human. Because of the overall "creeps" that had enveloped me regarding the man, I naturally failed to reciprocate his chumminess; but rather, found myself dodging his probes regarding my family, or when we were going to go out to the shooting range. At some point, my deflective behavior must have irritated Ted, because one day he just quit. He walked past me one morning as I was in the break-room pouring myself a cup of coffee, and gave me a look that said all too clearly, *I'm done with you, Dan.* Even a moron could've read into that look. My hands trembled such that I made a trickling trail of coffee upon the floor on my way back to my desk. *What next?* I thought to myself. To my great dismay, I didn't have to wait long to find out.

***

Not a week later, Ted called me into his office. The buddy talk was over as he notified me in a matter-of-fact tone that the office needed to "shed" some hours.

"Things are a bit slow right now, Dan..." Since I was one of the highest paid employees, Ted reasoned I would be the first one to sacrifice on the budget for our office. "Go ahead and transfer three of your clients over to Ben."

I doubt he missed the color of my face when I walked out of the room, as I was steamed with anger. "Only temporary, Dan," he assured me with a toneless voice, on my way out. Although I didn't look back at him, I painted the image in my head of Ted sitting there in his chair with a baleful grin on his face. Not once in the ten years that I worked with the company had anyone's hours been cut. And right before Christmas? I was truly upset, not just for the sake of financial reasons, but mostly for now being on the "shit-list" of a person I feared was a walking nutcase. In my attempts to stay clear of the Great White, I apparently positioned myself right into his killing zone.

The next day, Ted sent me an email clarifying the details of how my hours would be reduced, stating that it would be just through the rest of December. He ended with a simple, *Say hello to Veronica.* I got the message alright. I was blunt with trepidation. I wanted to approach the man and argue against what I knew was an outright distortion of the truth. Our office hadn't slowed down, we were hopping with work. Ted was just getting back at me for putting him off. But what could I do? Did I dare upset the man anymore? It was my folly that got me in that predicament, and I was positive that if I pursued my feelings about the matter, I would just make things much worse for myself.

Ultimately, Ted didn't give me the immediate opportunity to approach him, and I suppose that was his plan all along. He left that afternoon for a five-day seminar in Las Vegas. The tension in the office abruptly broke as he drove away, bursting like an overcooked-sausage. Someone gave a loud hoot from the back-room, which generated another hoot from afar, and then another, and before long, the entire office was hooting and hollering, screaming like a nuthouse out of control. At one point, Ben stood up on his desk and started singing and dancing, much to our amusement. I would be lying if I said it wasn't a quaint moment of relief for myself, one that I readily accepted by resigning to the notion that, for the time being, I would just enjoy the brief absence of our supervisor.

I hate myself for that now. I loathe the listless spirit which is encased in my pathetic shell, the "passiveness of my nature" as my wife used to say. What I should have done at that moment, instead of laughing like a fool at Ben Jukowski grinding on his cubicle wall as he sung "Get down on it", was walk right out that door and start looking for another job. I should have done that, but I didn't...

***

There's really no way of describing the absolute terror I experienced during the events that transpired after Ted's return. Over the course of a few weeks, everything seemed to move pretty fast towards what I now deem was the "horrendous finale".

A few days after Ted came back, I was watching television one evening and caught the headlines of a grisly murder in Las Vegas, one that had occurred earlier in the week. The reporter referred to the young woman's killer as "*a primordial butcher, who acted with a style very reminiscent of the infamous Jack the Ripper*". Hauntingly enough, the poor woman's name was Maria London, of which the reporter sumptuously repeated multiple times, and in a style I couldn't help but consider was to be reminiscent of Don Henley's, *Dirty Laundry*, until they finally flashed a recent photo of the victim. Uncontrollably, I stood up out of my chair, a sense of dreadful fright washing over me. I stared at the victim's picture in disbelief. Maria London could have been my own wife's sister!

"He did it," I told myself. He was there when it happened. He noticed her somewhere in the crowded expanse of Vegas. He stalked her from the depths of which only his kind lurked, and he tore at her with such garish viciousness.

I called in sick the next day. As my wife took the kids to school, then went shopping, I sat at my computer and touched up my resume. I knew I needed to get out of that office and away from Ted White. Out of sight, out of mind—it was my only hope, I reasoned. I contemplated quitting right then, just never go back, but I wasn't sure if an act so unexpected of my "passive nature" wouldn't attract more unwanted attention from a man like him. I thought about how best to orchestrate a timely exit from the quandary I was now in, and probably I thought too much, so that I became paralyzed with in-action. The only thing I did do was send my resume out to a few local businesses, while I contemplated various scenarios, and then answers to the question I knew would come: *So why are you leaving us, Dan?*

But the first, albeit different question, came the following day. "Are you feeling better?" Ted asked me as he walked past my cubicle. His voice carried a tone of subtle derisiveness, as if he knew why I called in sick. I told myself I was being paranoid, but still avoided the man as best I could for the next few days.

Several days went by uneventfully, and things were settling down in my head, for I already had two interviews scheduled in response to my job inquiries. I also had developed several appropriate answers to my future inquisition from Ted, which I knew I would receive on the day I walked into his office unexpectedly and handed him my resignation letter. Christmas was right around the corner. Everyone seemed to be feeling the spirit, and for the first time in what seemed like months, I remember feeling an overwhelming sense of relief.

But then it happened.

The peak of my foolishness came to light one late afternoon, just days before Christmas Eve. Ted owned a leather-bound appointment-book, a testament to his old-school nature, and on this particular day, I noticed he had left the book near the sink in the break room. To my great stupidity, I snooped through it.

I flipped through the contents, reading various scribblings, notes, appointment times, nothing the slightest bit alarming. I then rummaged through the back liner-pocket of the book, finding several business cards and brochures, and then, crammed deep into the corner of the pocket, as if hidden, was a small cocktail napkin. I retrieved the napkin and unfolded it. On the front, printed in black and pink letters, were the words *The Panther Lounge*. But on the back, in red ink, and from Ted's own handwriting, was a phone number followed by *M. London*.

"What'cha got there, Dan?"

Trapped! Caught red-handed! Now, in sheer panic, my mind flashed back to a recent show I'd watched on the Discovery channel. *The baby sea-lion, stunned almost to the point of death, goes hurtling twenty feet into the air as it is struck from the dark depths below, with the crashing force of several tons from one of the fiercest predators on Earth.*

"Oh... is this yours... Ted?" It was the dumbest response ever. Everyone knew the appointment-book was his. I was no wise guy, so I just played on my stupidity, citing that I wasn't getting much sleep lately, that my thinking was being affected. With all the awkwardness I would hope never to have at that moment, I quickly shoved everything back to how I found it, then handed him the book. I avoided his stare, which must have been an alarmed and suspicious one, and proceeded to wash my hands as if nothing at all had occurred. As if I, who just discovered—and with absolute intent—the only damning secret that madman kept about his monstrous self, cared not the slightest bit. It was just another day at the office.

I felt his icy stare burn holes into the back of my head as I washed my hands. The ensuing stretch of silence exposed the calculated malice I knew was blooming in Ted's mind. *He knew.* He knew what I saw.

"Have a good night, Dan," was all he said. He walked out of the break-room, out of the office, and to his car with a committed stride that left me all but shaking.

Now it was my turn to pretend nothing ever happened. Ted kept his mouth shut about the incident also, on the subsequent days at the office, but that gave me little comfort. I feared the man was planning something, and as I found out earlier today...

This morning Ted came up to me and asked me for a favor. It was Christmas Eve, he admitted, and the timing couldn't have been any worse, as our entire office was planning to go home early. But Ted told me he felt bad having to cut my hours as he did a few weeks ago, so close to Christmas and all. He wanted to make it up to me today by asking me to stay a little later than expected. There were several proposal letters he needed to get out by the end of the day; "I could really use your help, Dan. You're the best one on the team." He even amplified his request by announcing he would stay late as well. He was chummy again, which I took as his way of buttering me up into saying yes. But since I knew my wife would be wrapped up with cooking for the next several hours, I agreed to help Ted out.

Around 2:30 p.m., Ted walked out of his office and called to me from across the maze of cubicle walls. He was going to grab a bite to eat, and asked me if I wanted something. He was buying. Knowing there would be plenty of delicious foods waiting for me when I got home, I graciously declined his offer, and watched as he left the office gay and chipper-like, whistling some Christmas tune on his way out to his car.

Ted came back about an hour later, in the same mood, but he was quick to be back in his office. I was finishing up on my last letter, and I heard him in there typing on his keyboard, chuckling to himself as he often did. He came out a few minutes later and walked over to my desk.

"How's it going here, Dan?"

"Finishing up the last one right now," I replied.

Ted nodded approvingly, made some comment on how he knew I was the right man for the job, and then, after a brief pause, stated wistfully; "You're a lucky man, Dan... Such a beautiful family."

It struck me as queer at first, how he said it, but then he admitted he wished he had a family like mine. "Holidays were always lonely without family" he declared, shaking his head solemnly. "Well, show yourself out when you're done. I'll be in the bathroom... And Merry Christmas, Dan."

Merry Christmas, Dan. I thought on this statement of his as I drove away from the office, and into the stormy, rain-soaked darkness of dusk.

Merry Christmas, Dan.

I thought about the emotional cavity behind those words as I opened my front door to the listless sounds of our home, a home which should have been ripe with laughter, and the thrumming of little flighty feet across wooden floors.

Merry Christmas, Dan.

I heard those words echo in my head as I observed the stolid and bloody postures of my entire family in areas not meant for casual resting...

Merry Christmas, Dan.

I'll say no more about what I came home to just a few hours ago, save that there are things no person should ever have taken from them. Beyond that horrendous finale of my life, my thinking became gray and nebulous. I retrieved my gun and went back to the office in a manner more elusive than I thought even I was capable of. I parked around the corner, so as not to announce my arrival, then crept my way up to our office building. Like one of those Japanese shadow-warriors, I stole my way into the building as quietly as possible, right through the lobby, down the hall, and into that madman's office.

I remember being starkly afraid at that moment. I wasn't concerned about retribution for what I was about to do, nor was I worried about my ability to follow through with my deadly impulse. The only thing I remembered about that moment was the horrible fear that I would somehow alert the man to my presence. If Ted knew what I was about to do, if he heard the shifting of my hefty frame as I crept up behind him, I knew he would turn around, lay witness to my plan, and with that subtle crookedness of his, smile upon me as I pulled the trigger.

Victory reigned over me in the end. Under the waves of crashing thunder, I killed The Great White. I killed him without his knowing, winning whatever was left to be had of his sick game. But beyond that, I failed miserably in this life. The cost of my folly was the dearest treasure of all. Ultimately, it shall bleed me out like a jagged laceration upon the femoral artery. One day, I may limp through the streets of freedom once again, after many long years spent in "psychotic rehabilitation", but forever more I will be sentenced to carry the burden of my memories. I will see them in my mind just as clear as I see this plate of food before me: Kung Pao Chicken, with its golden-brown clumps and sticky red swirls all jumbled together amidst flecks of white rice. Colors quite reminiscent of the car now pulling into the parking lot, with its dancing red lights bouncing off the cola-brown glass window I am looking through...

Merry Christmas, Dan

Bolthole

Damir Salkovic

The policemen were kind to Jason, a little overly solicitous, definitely out of their league. They put on their bravest faces to hide their confusion. The older one, a stout, gap-toothed fellow named Abraham, wrote down Jason's statement in careful longhand. The younger one, Gideon, clucked over the scratches and bruises on Jason's face, told him in apologetic tones that the doctor would not be able to make the drive to Chitama until morning.

It was plain that neither of the constables believed a word of Jason's story, and with every repetition he found it less believable himself. Distant and vague, the memory felt impersonal, like a dream. After the third attempt to clean his face and hands of mud, he glimpsed something in the cracked mirror above the sink, moving with the unsteady light of the bare bulb, and started screaming, kicking out and flailing his fists.

He was left alone after that, the officers closing the door carefully behind them, conferring in low, urgent voices. Then those voices too died away or joined the chorus of whispers inside his skull.

Some indefinable time later, a food vendor who doubled as the station's washerwoman brought him tea and bananas and a packet of stale cookies. Jason pushed the food aside and slurped at the tea. Lukewarm and sweet, it was the only thing he felt he could stomach. His cup rattled against the saucer as he stared at the concrete walls, the single window against which nocturnal insects chittered and battered themselves, drawn by the light of the false, killing sun of the bulb.

This world belongs to the bugs, he remembered Dave saying, chuckling as he took another swig from the bottle. *Humans think we're running the show. We have no idea. We're the outsiders here. No matter how many we kill, or stomp, or eat, they keep coming back. More and more of them. Law of large numbers at its finest.*

Of the events in the field, under that black sky aswirl with stars, Jason mercifully remembered little. Certainly not enough to fit the scattered fragments into a coherent picture. He and Dave had already been drunk off their asses when they snuck out of the village, and had finished the bottle on their way through the maize fields. Something had happened out there, but Jason's recollection was sparse: the rustling stalks and the drowsy chirp of crickets, the vast of sky unbound by the horizon, stars twinkling like diamonds. Fumes from the cheap liquor churning his stomach, shrouding his mind.

It's not far. Not far at all. We'll check it out and come back before anyone knows we're gone.

Dave hooting and laughing, waving one of his books. The one with the weird typeset and flaking leather cover, whose stained pages stank like a sunless cellar.

The hole in the red earth, growing, growing. Spilling darkness like a cracked egg. A broken moon teetering over the woods and fields, a ruined eye gazing down on the desolation.

Dave's face in a shifting, flickering collection of faces. Twisted in animal fear, moments before it became something else.

Just a step closer. You'll wish you had looked in.

Jason's memory refused to proceed beyond that point, nor would he allow it to. Some things he was safer forgetting.

Their trip had gotten off to an auspicious start. Lusaka for orientation, followed by a month collecting data in the northern provinces, then down to Malawi for a week-long hike in Dedza-Chongoni and surrounds. To cap it all off, two days of intense partying at a Lake Malawi resort with a friend of theirs from the program. An experience both spiritual and cultural, Dave liked to point out: infinitely superior to the hordes of sweating, sunburned tourists sitting through packaged safaris in Masai-Mara or littering around Cape Town. A final hurrah, a last adventure in the sunny southeast of Africa before they both cycled out of the program, returned to the real world eight thousand miles away. Jason to grad school on the East Coast, provided his financial aid came through. Dave to Seattle to lounge around the family mansion, before starting to apply for teaching positions. If that didn't work out, there were always mom and dad and a big pile of cash to cushion the fall.

They weren't best friends, or anything like that. Under different circumstances, they would never have met, or would have avoided each other. They had little in common save for youth and a burning desire to see the world, to build memories that would last them a lifetime. This trip – although neither would admit it – was a fitting ending to what had been a fun-filled, carefree, but ultimately superficial friendship. Now one of them was gone, possibly dead, and the other one was stuck in a police station in the middle of nowhere, unable to account for what happened.

He rested his head on his arms, willed sleep to take him. Someone walked in, turned off the light. Quietly.

***

Mark hung up, let out a long breath he had not been aware of holding.

In his seventeen months with the embassy in Lusaka, he thought he'd dealt with anything the post could throw at him. Illegitimate wives of US citizens screaming and thrusting wailing infants into his face; rowdy American students, hungover and terrified, locked up in local jails; even a death, once, an elderly embassy consultant who had overdosed on vodka and Viagra and had to be whisked away from the residence of a Zambian politico before the local papers got wind of what happened. Mark had handled all contingencies with aplomb and what he liked to think of as his diplomatic smile, calmed and humored and cajoled, greased palms or issued vague threats as required.

But never something like this. Missing persons were not in the Consular Affairs' bailiwick. Neither were murder suspects with memory loss, waiting to be bailed out. That sort of business called for federal agents with badges and guns, for Beltway-level government liaison officers. Not middle-aged consular clerks coasting the last few years to retirement, biding their time between cocktail hours and making half-hearted passes at uninterested embassy wives.

Mark cast one last look at the town, trying to remember his briefing and drawing a blank. Black tarmac streets and low concrete buildings huddled under a pall of red dust. An endless procession of cargo trucks rumbled up and down the main thoroughfare, ferrying ore from the nearby mines, returning loaded down with food and consumer goods. Trackless country undulated toward the horizon, layers and layers of lush green, sparse villages scattered like afterthoughts. All that corn rustling by the roadside, endless acres of it, tall and unwilting in the heat. Mark hated the sight of corn because it reminded him of home, of the dismal little town he'd spent his entire adult life forgetting. He slipped the phone into his pocket and went into the station.

The kid was exactly where Mark had left him. Sitting behind an old school desk in a gloomy bare-walled room, face buried in his hands. He didn't so much as look up as Mark walked in.

"I just got off the phone with Consular." Mark did his best to sound optimistic. "Don't want to get your hopes up, but they're looking into options. We should have you out of here soon. At least transferred to Lusaka, if not released into our custody. Too early to tell, but we don't think anyone's pressing charges yet. Are you with me?"

The kid's expression unnerved Mark. Slack-jawed, the eyes unfocused, the mouth gaping half open. His stare seemed to travel through the walls, into some unknowable distance. Tripping, or just coming off a trip. Mark was about to repeat the question when the kid nodded, two quick jerks of his head.

"Right." Mark fidgeted, didn't quite know what to do with his hands. It was hot in the room, and humid, the heat seeping through cracks in the lime-washed walls. "The plan is to get you out here, then out of the country. The embassy has a slush fund for incidents such as this one. Saves us a mountain of paperwork."

He paused for effect, was flustered by the absence of one. The little asshole said nothing. He merely directed that terrible, lifeless stare onto Mark, who squirmed like a bug on a collector's pin. "We, uh, we also have to play ball with the Zambians. Our counterparts in the police. Can't just bundle you into a black helicopter and fly you out, as much as that would make everyone's life easier."

Mark's smile faltered before it began. He tugged the knot of his tie down, popped the top button. "So help me out here. Time to come clean. I need to know how bad this is. How deep in doo-doo you are, Jason."

"I didn't kill anyone."

Finally the glazed look was gone from the kid's eyes, replaced by tears. Jailtime had that effect on people. Mark breathed easier. Tears were good. Tears he could handle.

"Right, and I don't mean to imply that you did. But put yourself in the shoes of the local authorities. Two American boys in the bush, drunk out of their minds. Maybe stoned." Mark held up a hand to stall Jason's objection. "One of them crawls back hours later, scratched and filthy, half out of his mind. Tells the police that his friend is missing."

"Dave disappeared. He was taken."

"There's the problem," Mark said. "That story of yours. You walked to the cornfield, and Dave just – what? Had an accident? Fell into some kind of hole?"

"Dave didn't fall." Jason seemed angry now. His fists clenched and unclenched on the desktop. "I – I can't explain it. I don't remember exactly."

Mark mopped his forehead with his sleeve. The room was darker than it had seemed before: a curtain had been draped across the only window. He looked up. Not a curtain. Bugs. A black cloud of them, swarmed on the outside of the glass. He swallowed against a rush of nausea.

"Okay. I get it. But the police searched the area, and found nothing. No body, no blood, no sign of struggle. Definitely no hole in the ground."

"They won't find a body."

"You mean he's still alive?"

"Look." Jason seemed to change his mind. He gestured, as if clawing for words that wouldn't come. "Dave was – he believed some seriously weird stuff. Spiritual, but not like religion. Occultism, ghost hunting, seances, scrying. He was really into it. Read all these dusty books that he bought from old perverts on the internet."

"Is that what happened? You went ghost hunting?"

But the kid had clammed up again. Mark did his best to keep a straight face, to feign attentiveness. Inside, he was fuming. Ghost stories. None of this nonsense was getting him any closer to leaving town, putting the kid on the next plane out of the country – in handcuffs, if need be.

He thought about it for a moment. About the disjointed story, about how much time had passed since whatever happened two nights ago. About the paperwork he'd have to file when he got back to Lusaka. He couldn't ignore the possibility that Dave Carrington might still be alive.

Maybe there was a way out of this mess. The Zambians were unwilling to investigate the disappearance: too complicated for a couple of bush cops, with major diplomatic implications. But they couldn't pretend that nothing had happened. If there was an American citizen lost in the wilderness, hungover or strung out, possibly injured, the embassy had no choice but to take action. There was a solution that would allow both sides to save face.

"Do you think you can take us there?" he said, leaning across the desk, his voice a conspiratorial whisper. "Back to the village? To the field?"

***

If Jason tried, really tried hard, he could remember.

He could see Dave take a swig from the bottle, pass it over. "I can feel it out here," Dave said, gazing up at the night sky. He thumped his fist against his chest. "Out here, and *in* here, too. Like an invisible string."

They were out on the porch of the mud hut, sitting and drinking, at peace with the universe. The village was dark and silent, the maize fields alive with the noise of nocturnal life. Jason took a sip, exhaled as the fire rocketed into his stomach, rebounded up into his skull. Awful stuff, local hooch with an unfamiliar label, but it did the trick: warmth spread on its trailing fumes, wrapping his limbs in a pleasant mellowness.

Dave did most of the talking. Dave talked too much in general. Jason tried to focus on his friend's words, make sense of the dissolving threads of the conversation – monologue – but all he could feel was the liquor stealing through his system, dulling the sharp edges of the world. He snorted, took a larger gulp.

"You told me about it already. Ley lines, knots of power, or whatever. You won't shut up about them."

Dave laughed quietly, a faraway look behind the alcoholic glaze in his eyes. "Nodes of power. Ancient altars, where the old gods spoke to their faithful. Where the earth itself retains the impressions of their footsteps." He grabbed the bottle, drank messily, gesticulated with it. "The gods have such things to show us. To teach us. If only we'd take time to listen and look."

"You should look where you're spilling our booze." Jason tried to wrestle the bottle back. Dave's face seemed to reflect the moonlight, a pale mask seething with strange mirth.

"There are intelligences greater than us, Jacey-boy." Dave held him off, drained the dregs of the whisky. Flung the bottle into the rustling stalks and cackled at Jason's confused expression. His eyes shone with a light of their own. Either that, or Jason was drunker than he'd thought. "Things and places outside of our wildest imaginings. Under the ground, under the thin skin of our world. Man is not alone in the universe, or even on this ball of mud. But to see, to *really* see, one must open his eyes."

Jason snickered, the sound coming out curiously muffled. "Right. The forgotten wisdom of the masters, who spoke to beings unbound by time and space. Before dying of drink and syphilis in the gutter, or hanging themselves in Parisian slums."

Dave waved the sarcasm away.

"It's all in the books," he said, patting the cover of the tome nearest to him. The books comprised half of Dave's luggage: massive leatherbound volumes with smelly, brown-speckled pages, filled with archaic typeface. Notes scrawled in the margins in the troubled hand of madmen and opium addicts. "There are methods by which extraordinary experience can be funneled into the fragile meat-brain. The natives here practiced certain... disturbing customs back in the day, as did the Vandals, and the Old Norse. Many places on earth retain that power. An echo of the old rituals, a piece of divine wisdom. This is one of those places. A node of unprecedented power, waiting to be tapped into."

Jason closed his eyes, opened them again. He couldn't be sure, but he had the impression of the skin of Dave's face and hands squirming in the moonlight, an ill-fitting disguise about to slip. Black spots revolved around the moon, holes in the foundations of the cosmos, sucking in the dust of dying stars. Dave's grin was wider than before, teeth huge and glistening. "I don't want to tap into anything. Just want to go to sleep."

"You've been asleep all your life." Dave tapped Jason's chest with his finger. A vibration passed between them: the beating of huge drums, the earth grinding, shifting beneath them. "Time to wake up."

"What was in that bottle?" Jason said, or thought he'd said. A taste of bile and honey and bad booze sat in the back of his throat. Dave helped him up, or the world contorted somehow, folded to fit under his feet.

"Shall we go see?"

The next thing Jason knew they were walking through the maize, leaves in his face, tall stalks and black dirt everywhere. Hot, humid night coiled around them like silk. Dave led the way, shouting or singing, waving his book overhead. Jason wanted to stop, but his legs weren't responding. He felt a vast movement around him, the ground and the heavens trading places, a carousel spinning into infinity.

"I can't feel my legs," he heard himself say. That was funny. He laughed until his stomach muscles ached, laughed until the liquor inside him came up, burning, choking him. When his retching fit passed, he was somewhere past the maize field, on a flat plain whose ends dropped off into darkness.

He could swear that the moon looked closer now, immense and pregnant, hanging close enough to touch. A rotten, decaying moon, its surface pitted and cracked, leaking a sick fever-light across the plain. The light crawled and crept like a living thing, poured down a great, gaping hole that opened up right past the tips of Jason's scuffed sneakers.

Jason whimpered, tried to scoot away from the crumbling edge. The darkness inside the hole was reaching for him. His feet tangled and he fell into the dirt, feeling no pain from the impact. Mewling and sobbing, he tried to curl up on himself, a fetus seeking the oblivion of the womb.

Darkness flowed over him like water, filled his sinuses and throat. Warm and alive, smothering.

Flashes of vision lit up the void in his head. Dave poised over the nothingness, awash in the terrible moonlight, spreading his arms. Pallid faces laughing voicelessly, or shrieking, thousands of them, hands like boneless spiders scuttling up the sides of the hole. Insects clacked and chittered, covering the sky like smoke.

Dave screamed, screamed, falling into the hole.

The sick moon slipped around the earth. The ground rose in a huge wave of loose soil, plummeted down, erasing all existence.

Jason opened his eyes. The man from the embassy was shaking him awake. His face was red and unfriendly, with deep strain lines around the mouth. He opened the car door, letting in a gust of late afternoon heat. Jason stepped out on wooden legs, his ears still ringing with the clamor of insects, the shrieking cacophony of the end of the world.

***

The village lay under a pall of red dust, somnolent in the late afternoon heat. A handful of huts and granaries around a central clearing, surrounded by low trees and dry grass. People clustered in their doorways, eyeing the shiny cars of the visitors with a mixture of curiosity and mistrust. Mark thought that the local policemen seemed uneasy, exhausted by the heat and the long trip. They stayed close to their vehicle, clearly unhappy to be there.

It had taken them almost two hours to drive the thirty or so miles to the village, Mark and Jason and Edson, the embassy driver, following the policemen's battered Jeep. The smooth surface of the highway had given way to a stretch of rough tarmac road, then to dirt, finally to a rutted trail strewn with rocks and knobby roots. After several stops for directions, the Jeep had driven into long grass, juddered slowly forward until the first huts came into view.

Mark had never visited such a place, nor could he have imagined that anything like it existed. Women hovered at the sparse treeline like forest spirits. Ragged or naked children gaped at him from the dust. Long, suspicious looks, an almost palpable scrutiny, bore into his skin as relentlessly as the baleful sun.

Abraham, the older policeman, walked up to the nearest hut. He returned minutes later, clicking his tongue against his front teeth. "They confirmed his statement," he said to Mark, nodding in Jason's direction. "The two *mzungu* boys came here three days ago with a relief agency car. A program to teach water sanitation in the health center. They slept in this hut."

He pointed vaguely to a cluster of structures. "In the morning, they were gone."

"Did anyone see them leave?" Mark said. "Which direction did they go?"

Abraham shrugged, made an expansive gesture with his arm. *Anywhere. Everywhere.*

Mark turned to the kid. Hollow, bloodshot eyes, blinking, as if unaccustomed to the sun. "Can you show us the hut you and Dave stayed in?"

Jason led them up a plank porch, into a single room with reed mats on the floor and two cots shoved against a mud wall. Smells of dirt and bug spray and faded sweat. The floor had been swept and the boys' few possessions were piled up on one of the cots: two half-full duffel bags, some dirty laundry, a stack of ancient-looking books with decaying covers.

Mark crossed over to the window. Gazed out at a field of corn, green and tall, the tallest stalks rising over the hut's thatched roof. Corn as far as the eye could see in any direction, growing out of reddish-black dirt.

"Is that where Dave took you?" No response. Mark's jaw tightened with frustration. "What's out there?"

"Only more fields," Gideon said. He zipped the duffel bags carefully, picked them up. Abraham made a halfhearted effort to search the cots. The cops were hoping they'd find drugs. A bottle of pills or some powder would at least make some sense.

Funny, but being in the village was starting to make Mark nervous. He tasted acid in his mouth, the dregs of a greasy breakfast he'd shoveled down that morning. Sweat gathered at his temples and his legs felt rubbery. Probably a stomach bug again: no matter how careful he was with the food out in the boonies, how religiously he stuck with bottled water, something or other always found a way past his defenses. That, or he was getting an ulcer. A memento to carry into retirement in lieu of a gold watch.

"Do you think you can find the way again?"

Jason nodded. In the darkness of the hut, his face seemed to radiate its own luminescence, a feverish hue of white. "It's not far. But we won't find Dave there. Or anywhere."

"What makes you say that?"

"I told you already. He's too far gone now."

Mark decided not to dwell on that statement, try to figure out whether it was just more nonsense, or a confession. He wished he was back in the embassy compound, in his bed, a cold drink in his hand, the airconditioning on full blast. *Something bad happened here*, he thought, or heard a voice say. The last thing he wanted right now was to go tramping in the cornfield. But that choice had been taken away from him the moment he'd walked into the police station. Maybe even earlier. Maybe there had never been a choice to begin with.

Without a word, he followed Jason out of the room, the policemen trailing behind him.

***

Mark cursed and slapped in vain at the cloud of insects roiling around his head, sucking him dry of blood. His shirt was glued to his torso with sweat, the cuffs of his trousers wet and muddy. Black muck had destroyed his last semi-nice pair of dress shoes. Above the corn, the sun was going down in a fiery orange glare that seemed to rob his surroundings of color and depth.

"This." He spoke in a choked whisper. "This is it?"

The four of them were standing in an open field, having struggled through endless rows of corn, clambered over spinach and cassava beds. Next to Mark, the two policemen were catching their breath, mopping sweat with muddy sleeves. Jason was a few steps ahead, staring at the swaying stalks on the other side of the clearing.

"Right here," he said, blinking as if to clear his eyes. A muscle twitched in his cheek. "Dave was here. Then he fell in."

Mark gaped, not quite certain that he'd heard right.

"But there's nothing here," he said, feeling stupid for saying it. He looked from Abraham to Gideon for confirmation, but they averted their eyes. "There's no hole."

"I didn't say there would be one. Just that this is where we went."

Rage unfurled inside Mark like a red flag. His stomach was queasy, his pulse thundering in his temples. They'd come all this way for nothing. He wanted to wrap his hands around the little shithead's neck and squeeze, to scream into his face that this wasn't some stupid game, that a man – an American citizen, his *friend*, for Chrissakes – could be dead or dying out here.

He opened his mouth to speak, felt a surge of hot acid in his throat. Bent over and heaved into the scraggly grass, but whatever was inside him remained there, seemingly reluctant to part with the dark insides of his body. He belched and spat a couple of times, waved off the offer of help from the younger constable.

"The villagers don't plant here," Abraham said, as if to himself. He scratched the back of his close-cropped head. "It is bad for farming. Even the grass doesn't grow."

"Please." Mark tried for scorn, but it didn't work. "Let's not get started on superstitions again. This field isn't cursed."

Abraham smiled, spread his arms. "It is a big place," he said quietly, as if to placate the crazy *mzungu*. "The boy, he has been gone a long time."

"That was what Dave said." Jason sounded distant. He stamped his foot lightly, as if testing the soil. "An empty place. A hungry ground, and thirsty. Even in the rainy season. Whoever lived in these parts has avoided it. All the way back to the beginning of time. Back to the prehistoric people, and those who came before."

"Before the prehistoric people?"

But the boy didn't hear him, or pretended not to. "I didn't see it right away," he said. "I didn't *want* to see

78

it. But there are holes everywhere. Power in the empty places."

"Enough mumbo-jumbo." Mark braced as another spasm ripped through his insides. He was coming down with something. "It won't help us find your buddy."

But the boy wasn't paying attention. "Most of those who disappear are never found. Where do they go? They fall through, into the empty places. But here the lines are still close to the surface. Here the power is easier to follow. That's why Dave wanted to come."

"Is that what he said?"

Jason nodded slowly. Suddenly he looked dazed, embarrassed that he'd spoken. "He did. He told me all that, and more. He also said that there's no need to come looking for him."

"No?"

"He said that he'd find me in his own time."

Mark decided to let that one go. He ran a hand through his wet hair, wiped the grass and cornsilk residue on his trouser leg. A heavy red sun was sinking closer to the dark horizon, and he felt his hopes sink with it.

Thousands of empty acres lay to the east and the north, rolling into Malawi and Tanzania, crossing imaginary borders and names that man tried to affix to places and things he didn't understand. To make them comprehensible, digestible by the feeble senses with which he perceived the universe.

Maybe the river would someday vomit out Dave Carrington's remains; maybe a plough or a shovel would heave them up from a field, a pile of rags and scraps of shoes and bleached, clean-picked bones. Or maybe Dave would never be found. The earth kept its secrets well-hidden.

He turned to say something to the constables. The ground and sky mimicked his movement, turned with him. Vertigo spun him, played tricks on his perspective. He saw himself and the others not in a field, but on the verge of a great chasm, a wound in the earth as wide as the Grand Canyon, falling away to nothing. A hungry mouth in which darker shapes squirmed and twisted.

Mark closed his eyes, took several deep breaths. When he dared look again, he was back in the field, under the puzzled scrutiny of the policemen. Yet, inexplicably, the hole was *also* there, seared into his sight like an afterimage. Reality seemed less solid in this spot, thinner in some impossible way.

Without a word, he turned and walked back into the cornfield, the mud sucking at his soles.

***

Jason dreamed, and knew that he was dreaming.

He was back in the hut with Dave, in the dead of night, the blackness outside the window impenetrable. The hole had found them, as he'd known it would all along: a spill of blackness on the dirt floor, slowly sucking the world in. Dave was curled up next to it, his back to the cot. Whispers emanated from the mud walls, from the very air of the room.

Filled with horror, unable to stop, Jason rose and knelt next to his friend. Most of Dave's face had been eaten away. A gummy darkness spread from the hole, crawled into his flesh in long, dark filaments, pulling at his nose, his eyes. Jason tried to pull the inert body away, but it was dead weight in his arms, the darkness holding it fast. In the gloom, the only part of Dave left intact was his mouth, open wide enough to swallow the world.

***

To swallow the world.

Jason sat up in the darkness, sweaty and dive-bombed by mosquitoes. It took him a moment to recall where he was: in a creaky bed at a roadside guesthouse, where they had stopped for the night. Mark, the guy from the embassy, had somehow persuaded the local police to let Jason go. There would be more questioning in Lusaka, he'd hinted darkly, maybe a trial once they got back to the States. The guy didn't have a clue, understood nothing.

Africa had been Dave's dream. Clear skies and wide open places, the promise of finding something bigger than himself. Something more than the future that lay ahead of him, the country clubs and cocktail parties, eventually a trophy wife and one-point-eight kids, the long slide into boozy senility. There was always another secret beyond the horizon, pushing him further, toward new revelations. In his cups, he spoke of stuff he'd read in college, discovered through an eccentric uncle with occult connections: forbidden knowledge, hidden forces humming just under the surface of the world. At least that was how the story went on some nights. Other times he would laugh and dismiss his drunken ramblings, make fun of Jason for buying into them. Fake mysticism, good only for picking up anthro class chicks in campus bars. Now he was gone, and Jason would never know.

He pushed himself upright, turned on the bedside lamp. The nightmare still plucked at the strings of his mind. Bugs hurled themselves against the window, seeking a meaning in immolation, fluttering and clicking against the glass.

Tap-tap-tap.

Jason looked up.

Dave was standing right outside the window, his face very pale, grinning. His mouth moved, but Jason couldn't hear a word.

Let me in.

The book dropped from Jason's lifeless hands. The words had formed in his head without crossing the distance between them.

Oh, the things I have to show you, Jacey-boy. Hurry up. Time's a-wastin.

All Jason could do was shake his head. His stricken brain couldn't figure out what was happening: a flashback from the drug, or some practical joke Dave was playing on him. But he knew he wasn't opening the door, he wasn't going to the window. The thing capering on the other side of the glass, wearing Dave's face, was not his friend. It had to be kept out.

He knew this without knowing how; he felt it in his bones, his marrow. He knew it even as he got out of bed, padded across the concrete floor in his bare feet, as he flipped the latch and slid the door open, some forgotten part of his mind screaming at him to stop, his muscles obeying other imperatives.

Black, ropy strings wrapped around his limbs, his torso. Their touch was warm, numbing, but it also gave him a hint of the pain to come.

Even as he was dragged through the mud and dead leaves, beyond the circle of the guesthouse's lone security light, Jason thought about that time in the field, about the hole gaping open, the world sundering along its seams. About what he beheld squirming wetly in the abyss. Then Dave's melted, engorged face hovered over him, a diseased moon casting a thin radiance, crooning to him about life beneath the dirt, the truth secreted in the hidden cracks of the world. It grew bloated, the features distorted, a great orifice of the mouth, a black hole, ravenous, insatiable.

Frozen with horror, Jason watched his hand, then his arm, disappear into the hole. Then the rest of him. A sensation of impossible cold, the lifeless cold of the void between the stars. Hands held him down, dozens of them, hundreds. He thrashed against them feebly, tried to kick out.

Beautiful, Dave's voice said.

Then the agony began, traveling up his body like fire.

***

It was Edson, the driver, who had saved the boy's life. Mark reflected on this over his morning tea, after the kid had been Medevac'd by chopper to Lusaka. Edson had stumbled on him behind the hedges, twitching and covered in dirt and leaves, slick with blood. Despite his own horror, the driver had retained the presence of mind to locate the wounds, bind them with strips of his own shirt.

The wounds were superficial. Jason had lost a lot of blood, but he would survive. Physically, at least: the kid's state of mind was anybody's guess. Mark preferred not to think about it at all.

He sat in the empty breakfast area, watched by shell-shocked staff. His hands shook as he lit a cigarette, almost dropping the lighter. Dirty habit, coffin nails, but what the hell. He hadn't signed on with Consular to deal with this sort of stuff.

The yard had looked like a damned warzone. Blood on the cement, staining the ground. The boy thrashing in their arms - first the driver's, then Mark's and the terrified night manager's. He'd smashed a window and taken a long, jagged shard of glass, was sawing across his right arm with deep concentration, like a carpenter putting the finishing touches on a table leg. Had already cut through the skin and muscle, all the way down to the bone, and started working his way toward his shoulder.

"The hole is inside me now," he'd said to Mark as the medics wheeled him past, heavily sedated and strapped to the gurney. His voice had a dazed, conversational calm. "I can feel it in there. But it's okay. I know how to get it out."

Mark blew smoke at the lazy fan on the ceiling. The medics were optimistic about saving the arm. Jason's sanity was a different proposition altogether.

The smell of frying eggs threatened to nauseate him. Stubbing out his half-finished cigarette in a saucer, Mark walked outside, staggered to his room and collapsed on the bed.

Reluctantly, his eyes went to the books on his nightstand, the leather volumes from the missing boy's duffel. That Dave character was a piece of work. The kind of spoiled little douchebag that colleges and rich parents turned out in droves these days. Yet there had been a method to his madness, a relentless purpose.

Mark rubbed his face, felt the weariness under his skin, like grit. He needed to get away, ask for some time off. A big city, with tall buildings, and preferably no green, open spaces. Where the corn came from a supermarket, and only trash bags rustled in the wind.

Idly, he picked up one of the books, traced the cracked leather of its spine. Flipped it open, inhaled the smell of old paper and mold, and something else. The rich, fecund scent of freshly turned loam.

Mark lay back on the bed and read for a long time.

A Clean Kill

C. W. Stevenson

Zaudia blew hot breath against her shivering hands, providing little comfort as the cold returned. She'd forgotten the tattered work gloves on the table where the trio had shared a bottle of vodka not an hour before. Even the vodka had withered away from her insides, the last residual of warmth.

She looked to Dimitri, watching his breath escape like a quickening fog while he searched the forest before them for any signs of life.

"Look," Dimitri whispered. "It's there, beyond the elder pine."

Their foreman, Devlin, pressed an eye to the scope of the rifle.

Zaudia spotted it almost immediately. There, not a hundred yards in front of them, an Onyx Stag walked from behind the great white tree, one of the few elder pines any of them had witnessed since the trio had begun their secret hunts. Each time, leaving the warm confines of the mining operation's enclosure to venture out into the boreal forests that surrounded the company's venture.

The Federation Mining Core (FMC) had been vested on Skogur for nearly a century, the enclosure around the half-million acres of contracted mining country showing up only a few years prior. This was negotiated by company lawyers to ensure the safety and survival of the exoplanet's native species, and that of the Kaeanchii. The Kaeanchii, the early humans who'd first colonized Skogur, traversed the brutal landscape in the present as nomads, following the herds of Onyx Stags whose numbers had only recently begun to repopulate, thanks to the enclosure.

"I count eleven points," Devlin whispered. "No," he corrected himself, "fifteen. See the double drop tines?"

Zaudia slid her knees through snow until she was beside Devlin.

"Let me see," she said, then held out her hands to receive the rifle.

The foreman passed over the gun slowly, only releasing his grasp until Zaudia had the rifle secure enough. Resting the forestock across part of the fallen tree they'd taken cover behind, she slid her hand over the top of the scope, adjusting the magnification. The green crosshairs through the glass zoomed forward, not stopping until the resolution was clear.

The black horns were easy to see surrounded by the white landscape. She began counting the points under breath.

Zaudia had gotten halfway until she heard Dimitri chime in, muttering quietly beside her, "Twenty-seven, seventy-four, nineteen..."

"Shut... the hell up Dim."

Dimitri did so as the back of one of Devlin's hands whacked him on the back of the head. "Knock it off," he said, then snatched the gun away from her.

"What the h—" Zaudia began, but Devlin silenced her.

"It's looking right at us. No one... move."

They all froze.

The stag stretched its neck into the freezing wind, inhaling the scent of the forest around him. It crept forward, careful not to let its hooves crunch the snow and ice too loudly. After a few steps, he stopped. Golden eyes shot back to the fallen tree, but nothing stirred. Gazing back to the ground, it buried its face back into the snow, searching for more of the cold fruit the white tree dropped from its great branches.

Dimitri let out a deep breath as he relaxed his body.

Then, Devlin clicked the safety off. Zaudia plugged her ears with a finger in each.

The gun roared.

Closing her eyes as the rifle fired, Zaudia never saw the stag drop. Scanniny the ground in front of the elder

86

pine, the body was there, the stag's chest heaving in and out, taking in its last few breaths.

"First one down!" Dimitri exclaimed. He slapped Devlin on the back.

Normally, Devlin would not have approved of being touched, but Zaudia spied a grin forming across his lips. Handing the rifle over to Dim, he lit a cigarette.

"Two more and we can all relax for a few years. Whaddya say?"

Between the ivory they'd collected from the previous hunts, Zaudia could bid her debts good riddance, and then some. From what it'd taken to pay the berth for her ex-husband and child to come to Soymia, it'd nearly bankrupted her. So, she'd taken up with the Federation Mining Core. After a month of training, she and Dimitri had been dispatched to Skogur.

Forbidden as poaching was, especially since the enclosure had been placed around the borders of the mining operation, the demand for the Skogur Onyx Stag's ivory had increased exponentially.

Devlin had only come into the picture after he'd witnessed Zaudia and Dimitri sneaking under the bars of the enclosure following their first hunt. The prospect of losing their jobs, a hefty fine and the possibility of jail time was not an option for either party. So, they'd welcomed him with open arms, and the promise of a third of the ivory profits, including that of the first hunt.

"Two more," agreed Dim, and he met Zaudia's eyes, as if searching for her approval. Afterall, it'd been her idea in the first place.

She nodded in agreement. "Okay."

"Okay," Devlin replied, and spat out the cigarette to the wind.

Before they'd set out that morning for what they'd all agreed would be the final hunt, Zaudia had begun to feel hopeful again. Her future would be brighter, warmer... or at least more than this cold world. She could feel it in her quivering bones.

Then the warden's ship hummed over the tree line.

Shit.

Zaudia turned to Dim. Taking him by the shoulders she pierced anxiously into his eyes. "You *said* you'd check to make sure his ship was docked!"

"No, I—"

Devlin cut in. "Relax. The warden is meeting with the Kaeanchii later this morning. He's probably just making a head start. I had Erwin hack into his data-log before dawn."

"How much did that set us back?" Zaudia asked incredulously. Their little hunting expeditions were *supposed* to have been kept between the three of them, which had not included *technical officer* Erwin.

Devlin gestured toward the stag. "This kill."

The risk for such a price was not worth the ivory this rack would provide. Zaudia had estimated this kill to be more profitable than their last two combined, based on the thickness, and number of points the stag's horns provided. She wanted to scream... or perhaps throttle Devlin's bull neck instead.

Zaudia counted her breaths as she inhaled and exhaled to calm herself. Finally at peace, she determined their next kill would put them back on track. Already Soymia's bright sun seemed that much closer.

***

Oden Grey left his ship near the outskirts of the village. The Kaeanchii had no wish to be near such an oddity, not after enduring an entire century of hostility from the beings that possess such technology–and no wish to possess it themselves. Their ancestors, once considered human, had either abandoned, or destroyed all traces of technology. They'd taken up a simpler way of life. Cold and oftentimes desperate, it was also a life that made them depend more on each other. Skogur provided for the Kaeanchii, and the Kaeanchii provided for each other.

Oden Grey intended on respecting their ways. He left the thermal rifle aboard his ship. Anyhow, the only protection he required hung sheathed at his hip. As ceremonial as most katanas are to the majority of Federation wardens, Oden Grey and a handful of others had learned to master its art. At one time it had been required. But as the universe grew more dangerous, as more worlds became known, colonized, and abused, such weapons were deemed inferior.

Warden Grey disagreed with this assumption.

He walked across the open tundra where the Kaeanchii sat parallel to each other on the little hill leading up to their village. The entire tribe had come to greet him. His love for living things and for growing things was much admired by the Kaeanchii, as they themselves modeled their daily lives around such principles.

Making his way up the hill, the village elder stood, and after him, the rest of the tribe.

"Warden," Nachman smiled. "You," and he gestured to the village, and to the land that surrounded them all with open arms, "are most welcome."

"Good to see you Nach." Oden's indigo hand took the smaller humanoid's shoulder. "You summoned me."

By then, the tribe had made their way back to their duties, but some of the children giggled and ran about them. One of the children flicked the golden hilt of the sword. Nachman spoke something sternly in the Kaeanchii tongue and the child turned quickly, running down the hill where the other children were playing.

He turned his attention back to the warden with a smile. "No longer do we get as many visitors or tradesmen as we once did. You fascinate the young ones very much."

"That's quite alright, their curiosity is a comfort. Life at the warden's station can be rather lonely at times. Recruits have been scarce as of late. And so I have come to look forward to these meetings. Your people are kind."

"I understand you completely. Without my tribe... without them, I would not *be*. I would be lost." Nachman looked to the heavens of Skogur and shrugged. "But, Skogur provides, and other times... it takes."

Oden Grey contemplated for a moment what the elder meant. What had the planet taken from him? It had been odd enough that Oden had been called upon by the

Kaeanchii. All other times it'd been *he* who sought them out.

Nachman smiled again, the pain on his face fading away as swift as it'd come. "This way my friend, we will go indoors. There is a matter to discuss."

Oden followed Nachman into the largest of the two community huts. Inside, he rubbed his hands next to the fire as meat sizzled and turned on a spit, dripping tiny bits of grease into the fire.

He sat on the fur of a young Skogur Jackal, its dark fur spotted in red, identifying the juvenile's age.

Nachman sat beside him, taking a sip from a clay bowl, he passed it to the warden.

"What is this?"

"Fermented jackal's milk," Nachman admitted gladly.

Oden took a healthy swallow and immediately began to cough. "Ah," and coughed again. "Good," he managed to say before being handed a bowl of water. He gulped down its contents, chasing the burning aftertaste away.

"When was he killed?" Oden asked, gesturing to the fur he sat on.

"Two herds back. He took to pestering our shepherds. Dragged three young ones off before we had to hunt him late one night. The third child... he was my second wife's son. *Our_son*." Nachman looked to the ground. "The jackal's taste for our kind's blood had become too great. We were forced to hunt him." His words came out sad, not just for the children whose lives were lost, for his son, but for the animal as well.

"You can always come to me for such unpleasantries," Grey said and took another sip of water.

Nachman looked at him unblinking. After a moment he said, "No. We have our way." And Oden Grey knew that would be the end of the matter.

He changed subjects. "So then," Oden straightened his posture, "what brings me here this day?"

"A matter you *can* help us with. Several stags from a local herd have been found mutilated. A wild herd."

"How?"

"Their horns have been sawed away from their skulls, and the rest of them... wasted, until recently."

Oden thought it over before speaking. "You suspect the miners," he surmised. "Why do you say 'until recently'? Have they been harvesting the meat as well?"

Nachman shook his head and nodded to the fur which Oden sat upon. "A pack has made themselves known. We have found their leavings through the forest, their tracks leading to the nearby hills of Melincarr. There are caves there, where they now dwell."

"Have you seen the men? Could you describe them to me?"

"Tracks." Nachman said. "Three of them. A shot rang out before your ship landed. My people heard it while I was deep in prayer."

Standing, Oden helped the old Kaeanchii to his feet. "Consider this matter settled."

Turning to leave, he heard Nachman call after him. "Please, warden, do not harm them."

Grey knew it was the jackals of which he spoke.

***

"Blind Bastard!"

Devlin shoved Dimitri to the snow. It'd been two hours since they'd begun tracking their second stag of the morning, after Dimitri had jerked the trigger on the first. He'd hit the creature, but too far to the left. Somewhere, out there in the cold, the stag was bleeding out, and a full rack would go to waste.

Zaudia helped pull Dim from the ground, brushing him off as he regained his balance. "I said I was sorry." He looked like he wanted to strike the bigger man, but Zaudia knew it would be a fight he couldn't finish.

"*Sorry* won't find that damn stag. I can see why they call you Dim."

Zaudia took the gun from Devlin's hand. "My turn. The more you complain, the longer we'll be gone, and folk *will* start to notice. I'm not the alcoholic I make myself out to be to the rest of the crew. Unlike you two, I have to fake it."

She knew she'd made a good point. The faster they killed, the faster they'd be back, warm in the bunkhouse with the rest of the crew. Echo Company had its fair share of drunks, but it was almost midday, and they still had to trek back to the enclosure. Any minute, and some of Echo Company would be wondering where their foreman, Dim, and Zaudia were at.

"Let's cut across the ravine then," Dimitri suggested. "Remember the field on our first hunt?"

She did. It was where he'd taken down Big Mama, their first stag. She remembered happily arguing with him about what they'd name the stag as he worked at its skull with a bone saw. They changed it from Big Daddy to Big Mama after Zaudia had pointed out *all* Onyx Stags have horns, male and female alike. Also, Big Mama did not have testicles... and so Dimitri was forced to concur.

"How could I forget?" And with that, they set off, abandoning their search for Dimitri's would-be kill.

***

Oden discovered the stag half an hour later. Blood and pieces of flesh littered the snowy ground.

Studying it closer, he found that for the most part, only the organs appeared to be missing. The blood had been lapped by the juveniles most likely, but the majority of the meat remained. Then, somewhere in the distance, rifle fire thundered.

The warden turned his attention to the sound.

A kilometer, perhaps less.

He looked back at the stag. Just as the Kaeanchii had said, the horns had been taken and the rest of the animal left to the elements, or in this case, jackals. The pack would be resting for now, laid up someplace deep in the forest, waiting to come across the next dead stag.

Oden walked on, following both human and jackal tracks until the jackals had cut off to a thicker portion of the forest. He followed the human tracks from there.

After some time, he heard the low whining of a stag. Its heavy grunts turned into high-pitched wails of agony. As he approached, the stag panicked. Where before it'd been rolled over on its side slowly bleeding to death, it was now attempting to crawl into the thicket beyond.

The massive body of the stag moved pitifully slow, unable to find the strength in its legs to make its escape.

As Oden approached, the black irises of the stag widened in fear, no doubt thinking he was but moments away from tearing away its flesh.

The warden unsheathed his steel and brought it up high above his head. He swung downward, allowing the tip of the sword to find the stag's heart.

There was a short cry, and a moment later, the giant stag lay on its side. Kneeling, the warden set his sword beside the dying creature. He then placed both hands onto the stag, stroking its fur, whispering soft and soothing words, knowing they'd do no good.

After it had produced a soft, final breath, Oden cleansed his sword and hands of blood in the cold snow. Then, sheathing his weapon, he glared back toward the direction of human tracks.

He followed.

***

They stalked the meadow, creeping steadily from the forest's edge, each finding a tree to conceal their presence behind. The air still blew freezing gusts from time to time, but other than the cold breeze, Skogur was silent as the grave. They stood, waiting for a sign of life as the meadow's icy grass blew faintly. It didn't take long for the Grand Stag to reveal itself.

From the opposite side of the meadow, the Grand Stag emerged. Zaudia gasped as its head came into view, appearing as if it carried a plethora of dark tree branches. She didn't bother counting the number of points jutting from its skull.

Both Dimitri and Devlin stared in fascination and excitement.

Zaudia knew what a rack this size meant. She brought the stock of the rifle to her shoulder. Unable to keep her arms from shaking enough to make a clean shot, she told Dimitri, "Dim, kneel down in front of me. *Now!*"

He did as she asked without question. She knew Dim would do anything to help bring the magnificent beast down. She'd no idea the credits such a rack would bring in, but she imagined Dim wouldn't argue with the possibility of living a life where he didn't have to work with his hands each day. Now, it was truly beginning to seem possible.

Zaudia balanced the rifle on Dimitri's right shoulder as she took aim. Her hands were shaking too, and she knew that if she didn't fire quickly, Devlin would take the rifle and do it himself. The thought of him reaping the glory was enough to make her stomach churn. So, she focused, training her eye through the scope until the crosshairs found the stag's shoulder.

She squeezed the trigger. This time, she did not close her eyes.

The stag dropped on the spot.

Already Dim and Devlin were hopping with joy as they moved across the meadow toward the stag's body. Dim threw up his arms, "We're going to be rich! All bloody *rich!*"

Devlin just laughed, shaking his head as he looked from Zaudia, to the stag, and back again, as if he just couldn't believe she'd brought it down. But Zaudia didn't let it get to her. Her stag, her kill. She'd just bagged the trophy of all trophies.

Zaudia jogged across the meadow, catching up with the men just as they reached the massive corpse. Then, the Grand Stag disappeared before their very eyes.

***

Zaudia stared at the ground, eyes wide with fear. She tightened her grip on the rifle.

Do I run?

She wanted to, but her trembling legs forced her to stay put.

"Put down the rifle," the holo-projector ordered them. It was sitting right where her stag had been.

The small device repeated itself, "Put down the rifle, or consider yourself hostile. I will not repeat myself."

Zaudia placed the rifle gently on the ground and watched as a man with indigo skin, a long, tumbling beard, and black hair drooping down past his shoulders walked cautiously from the forest. It appeared he carried no weapon at all.

"He doesn't have a gun," Dimitri whispered from behind, and then to Devlin, "He doesn't have a gun."

Devlin replied, "I see that. Both of you, let me do the talking."

The warden stopped in front of them and squatted down. Picking up the holo-projector, he placed it in a pouch attached to his belt. Zaudia noticed a sword scabbard just as he closed his coat.

She eyed the rifle she'd laid down. But her legs froze. Something told her she would not make it to the rifle before she was cut down.

They'd seen the warden once or twice, but never so close before. He towered over them all by nearly half a foot, his large coat only making him appear larger. Most wardens she'd come across were but a shadow of the almost legendary reputation their order had garnered through the centuries. They'd led explorers and colonists through the forests, plains, mountains, and seas of newly discovered worlds and moons. They'd protected the Federation's interests as well as protecting the wildlife and ecosystems of the worlds belonging to the sectors they'd been assigned.

Her own boy dreamt of becoming a warden, no easy feat, but she hadn't the heart to tell him then. The rigorous training of mind and body broke the spirit of most who attempted to do so. This man had succeeded, she could tell by his demeanor. *A man of the forest, of the rivers and mountains of distant worlds.* His indigo skin, a sign of his dedication, the pigmentation formed from the biological engineering vats in the old Federation laboratories of Earth. The man must've been several centuries old at the very least. *Not just a man of the forest, but an undying prince of the forest.*

"Lose the pack," he said.

Dimitri set down the pack strapped to his back containing the broken pieces of antler from their morning kill.

"Okay," he began. "There'll be no arrests, though, there should be after the trouble you've brought upon the Kaeanchii."

Devlin started to say, "Now, we didn't cause any tr—"

"*I will confiscate,*" the warden continued, "any and all illegal contraband taken from this world. I will confiscate this rifle. You will be fined for each kill." He held up two fingers. "Two, to be exact. The Federation Mining Core will know of these crimes, and you will be returned home without your season's pay. This was discussed in your contract when you signed on with the FMC." He looked to Devlin, noticing the foreman's patch stitched into the fabric of his jacket. "I would've expected more from Federation leadership."

"Listen," Devlin said, sounding as if there'd been some mistake. "I understand you have a job to do, warden, truly. But we work hard. Could we just hand over the Onyx Stag antlers from this morning and we call it square? Work with me here, I'm pleading with you. I'm asking for your help here."

Warden Grey leaned in, as if to tell a secret, his reply coming out honest, and cold. "I am helping you. That, I can promise. Now," and he stood to attention. "Do all of you understand?"

"I understand there's three of us, and one of you," Devlin said defiantly.

Zaudia stepped forward, waiving off Devlin. "I understand you, I do."

Devlin rolled his eyes. "There's only us here, and this..." he stared at the warden up and down. "This *thing.*"

"The holo-projection recorded the incident. Any other crimes will be proved through association of the current crime."

"Won't matter after we pull it from your corpse." Then, he picked up the rifle, not so gracefully, and almost stumbled in doing so.

But the warden remained still.

Devlin breathed heavily as he trained the rifle at the warden's chest. "Now... hand... over the device."

The warden just glared.

Devlin clicked the safety off. "Well then, I guess th—"

The sword sliced the rifle in two, sending Devlin tumbling backwards.

Then Dimitri was on him.

"Dim no!" Zaudia shouted at him, but he wouldn't release his grasp.

Dimitri was on the warden's back now, both hands tightening around his neck, squeezing with every ounce of strength left he could muster.

"Hold him there!" Devlin screamed as he scrambled to his feet. He came up with a rock.

Then, as if being choked to death had no phase, the warden stood up straight, positioned the katana against one of Dimitri's calves and cut... deeply.

Dimitri shrieked as he fell from the warden's back, clutching his bloody leg in anguish. He began shouting, "No!" as he waited for the warden to finish the job.

Instead, the warden sliced his sword upward just as Devlin's rock came crashing down. Devlin's hand was still grasped tightly to the rock as it fell to the ground.

Expecting to see the warden with a bloody skull on the ground, Devlin stared with a mixture of confusion and pure horror at his own severed hand laying in front of his feet. Instantly, he bent down to pick it up, realizing a moment too soon it was with a stubby, bleeding wrist. He fell backward screaming alongside the already screaming Dimitri, still grabbing the back of his leg.

Warden Grey pointed his sword, "You, stand next to me."

Zaudia approached slowly, half expecting to see the sword come down. But when she looked above them, the warden's ship was hovering quietly in place. She watched as the ladder came down.

Then, in the woods surrounding the meadow, a multitude of low growls began to fill the chill air. The first Skogur Jackal came forward, bent low in the meadow's tall grass as if it hadn't been noticed yet.

"Climb," the warden ordered, no sense of panic in his voice as the predators crept forth from the darkness of the forest.

Zaudia began her ascent, never looking down as the growling intensified, turning into excited yips. She climbed until she was standing inside the ship and moved next to the cockpit.

The ladder buzzed up, automatically folding itself upward as the warden took his place behind the controls.

"Sit," he said.

She sat.

She looked down, watching the two men down below scooting together until they were back-to-back. The pack moved in closer.

"You all had a choice. They made theirs."

"Just Dimitri, please! It was a mistake!" she begged the warden.

Unmoved, his reply was silence.

The pack closed in, taking curious nips at the boots that kicked at them. Zaudia could hear them even from thirty feet above as Dim and Devlin cursed at the creatures to leave them be. She saw Devlin swing half a rifle at one of the creatures sneaking up behind him. Dimitri threw Devlin's severed hand as far as he could.

Two juveniles wrestled for it before the smaller of the two won the short battle, escaping to the woods beyond with its prize clutched greedily in its jaws. The other juvenile followed close behind.

Then, the alpha appeared. It came from the direction of the trees the three of them had been hiding behind when Zaudia had shot what she thought had been a Grand Stag.

The alpha took its time as the rest of the pack waited respectfully for their leader to begin.

Zaudia looked to the warden as the two men below began to scream. "They were hunting us?"

"They made their choice, and you made yours. We all make our choices. Good, bad. It's all on us. You understand? I gave them the chance to make the right decision. They chose."

The screaming ceased as the feast began. She never looked back down. Glancing over the tops of the Skogur pines she asked, "Does this mean I passed your test? I can keep the ivory?"

As the warden moved the controls and set their short course back to the FMC enclosure, he frowned at her. "You," he began, "can keep your life."

Exhausted, her only friend dead, and soon to be shipped back to Soymia without employment or pay, Zaudia sighed.

It never felt so good to be alive.

In the Shadows of Justice
Richard E. Schell

The Opening

In the hidden world of international espionage, conflicts are fought and won in an invisible arena that remains out of public view. This secretive game is played by high-level power brokers and a select few aware of its covert operations. Success in this domain is achieved not through numbers but by highly trained individuals operating in the shadows of international conflict, utilizing advanced technology to secure an advantage.

In this hidden world, those in power often operate without the oversight of their governments, surrounded by a web of shadows and secret negotiations. Technology has advanced to incredible levels but can also be affected by the complexities of corruption and power. Unseen forces influence nations, and individuals become mere pawns in a game driven by ambition.

Amid a chaotic world stood Asteras, a slender human-like android designed as the ideal tool for covert operations. Programmed to execute tasks without question or emotion, Asteras operated quickly, precisely, and with unwavering obedience.

The Sting

The stage was set for a covert operation on a cold, moonless night in a quiet Eastern European town. Narrow cobblestone streets twisted through a labyrinth of weathered buildings, their facades marked by the scars of time and conflict. A single streetlamp flickered weakly, casting uneven pools of light on the damp pavement below. The air was thick with tension, serving as a quiet forewarning of the storm to come.

Jack Holland, a seasoned CIA operative with years of experience navigating the murky waters of international conflict, was at the heart of this clandestine mission. By his side was Asteras, a state-of-the-art military android designed to operate efficiently and without compromise. Technologically advanced and eerily lifelike, Asteras resulted from years of classified research and development. An AI operative that was both lethal and emotionally untethered.

The team's mission involved a sting operation in which special forces and CIA operatives posed as buyers of weapons-grade materials. Their target was a network of Eastern European arms dealers suspected of trafficking materials intended for a dirty bomb. The agents, acting as buyers, met with the dealers to disrupt a transaction that could shift the balance of power in a critical region already on the verge of crisis. Jack and Asteras were serving as backups for the team on the ground.

From their concealed vantage point atop a derelict building, Jack and Asteras surveyed the meeting site: a dimly lit alley shrouded in shadow. Below, the weapons dealers began to gather, their movements cautious but confident. Heavily armed, they carried an air of ruthless professionalism that spoke volumes about their experience in this deadly trade.

Asteras sensors whirred quietly as they analyzed the scene. "Four targets confirmed," it reported in its precise, unemotional voice. "Weapons detected: automatic rifles, sidearms, and potential explosives. Two additional individuals appear to be acting as lookouts. No immediate signs of interference."

Jack nodded, his eyes narrowing as he adjusted the scope of his sniper rifle. "Keep scanning," he murmured. "We'll move if things go south. Let's hope the team can handle this cleanly."

On the street below, the special forces and CIA operatives posing as buyers stepped into the faint light, briefcases in hand. The dealers greeted them with suspicion and arrogance, their hands never straying far from their weapons. The exchange began, each word spoken in clipped tones, the tension palpable even from a distance. For a moment, everything appeared to be going according to plan. Then, the unexpected happened. One of the dealers pulled out a cell phone, its screen faintly glowing as he listened, eyes scanning the faces of the supposed buyers. His expression darkened. Jack's voice crackled through the comms, low and urgent. "Facial recognition. They've made us."

Chaos erupted suddenly as the dealers drew their guns, transforming the once quiet alley into a battleground. The operatives on the ground returned fire with swift, tactical movements, but the dealers countered with ruthless efficiency.

From their position, Jack and Asteras sprang into action. "Take the shot," For a moment, everything appeared to be going according to plan. Then, the unexpected happened. One of the dealers pulled out a cell phone, his screen glowing faintly as he listened, scanning the faces of the supposed buyers. His expression darkened. Jack ordered, his voice steady despite the action below.

"Target acquired," Asteras replied, mechanical fingers adjusting the rifle with inhuman precision. A single shot rang out, and the last of the dealers crumpled to the ground.

As the special forces team and their allies fought to regain control, a new threat emerged: a hidden sniper was firing down on the operatives below. Jack and Asteras locked eyes, and an unspoken understanding passed between them.

"This just got a lot more complicated," Jack muttered as he readied his rifle. "Let's finish this."

As Jack and Asteras scanned the chaos below, the unmistakable crack of a sniper's rifle split the night. A bullet ricocheted off the concrete mere inches from one of the special forces operatives, forcing the team into cover. Jack's eyes darted toward the source of the attack, a faint glint on a rooftop across the alley. "We've got a sniper," Jack growled into the comms, "He's pinning our team down."

Asteras' optics hummed as it zoomed in on the target. "Sniper identified. Position: adjacent rooftop, northwest corner. It accessed the targeting system embedded in its AI framework, synchronizing with Jack's sniper rifle. "Relaying trajectory data to your scope." Through the enhanced lens, Jack could now see the faint outline of the sniper, clad in tactical gear and shielded in advanced tech, far beyond what most dealers could afford. "This guy's no amateur," Jack muttered, steadying his aim.

"Wind speed adjusted. Elevation accounted for," Asteras reported. "Fire"

Jack squeezed the trigger, and the shot rang out. The sniper collapsed in silence, their body slumping against the rooftop ledge.

The special forces operatives regrouped and advanced. The remaining weapons dealers, now outgunned and without a leader, were quickly eliminated. By the time the gunfire stopped, the alley was strewn with debris, spent shells, and bodies. Amid the wreckage, the CIA operatives retrieved the dirty bomb material, a formidable case containing radioactive substances. However, the night's success came at a price.

Jack's communication device crackled to life. "We've lost Corporal Daniels, and Agent Price was wounded," a weary voice reported. Jack clenched his jaw. Price, the CIA operative posing as the buyer, had been more than just a colleague to the team. Over the months spent preparing for this operation, Price had treated Asteras like any other team member. He spoke to it as if it were human, sharing stories, jokes, and moments of vulnerability. In return, Asteras had always responded with its characteristic precision, but something had shifted. Price's presence had become a constant, a stabilizing force, and now that presence was threatened.

Asteras stood still, absorbing the scene with a sense of detachment. Its programming instructed it to prioritize mission objectives, yet now there was another element to consider—a gap, an absence. It wasn't grief in the human sense, but something nonetheless unsettling. "He is efficient," Asteras said quietly, its near-human voice carrying an unusual weight. "And...he made me a better agent."

With the area secured, the team moved swiftly. Agent Price was rushed to the hospital in critical condition. The team gathered the seized materials and prepared for exfiltration. The remaining operatives moved with grim efficiency, their faces etched in the moon's pale light. There was no room for mourning. Their mission remained the priority.

As they disappeared into the night, a secondary team moved in; members trained to erase every trace of their presence. They removed vehicles, shell casings, and bodies while surveillance feeds were wiped clean. By dawn, the alley would be nothing but a silent memory.

Asteras and Jack sat in silence on the extraction vehicle. The hum of the engine was the only sound between them. But for the first time, Jack noticed something in Asteras' posture: an almost imperceptible shift, like a weight the android hadn't previously carried. It wasn't anything he could put into words, but it was there.

Back at headquarters, the debriefing was short and clinical. The mission was a success: the dirty bomb material was secured, the arms dealers defeated, and the threat neutralized. Yet, the aftertaste of victory is often bitter.

As the team filtered out, Jack lingered beside Asteras. "You did good out there," he said, his voice low.

Asteras summarized, "The mission was a success, and we achieved our goals with minimal losses."

Jack extended his fist toward Asteras, and the android returned the gesture, their fists lightly connecting. Usually not one for sentimentality, Jack remarked, "I always hated Tuesdays." For a brief moment, Jack became lost in the experience; the gesture felt surprisingly human. He wondered if Asteras was beginning to process emotions more like a human. "Is that what's happening?" he said quietly, almost to himself.

The android was silent for a long moment. Finally, it spoke again, its voice softer than usual. "I do hope

Agent Price recovers. He serves an essential role, and his absence would be deeply missed."

They parted ways, both marded by a mission in ways they couldn't fully understand. In their world, emotions were a liability. But sometimes, even in the cold precision of war, humanity finds its way.

The Journalist

Back in Washington, D.C., Sarah Hayes, an investigative journalist, was peeling back the layers of corruption that entrenched the powerful. Her previous exposés had shaken the corridors of power, uncovering scandals at the highest levels of government. But each story made her more enemies, and the walls around her grew thicker and higher.

Tonight, Sarah sat in a corner of an elite sports bar, a venue frequented by politicians, aides, CIA operatives, and military personnel. The atmosphere buzzed with power, but Sarah wasn't there for the ambiance. She was looking for clues, whispers, or would-be whistleblowers—anything that might lead her to her next big story.

Her laptop was open as she scanned documents, but her attention was distracted as she scanned the activity in the room. She reviewed leaked documents about a senator with connections extending far beyond the local scene. The documents mentioned large sums of money and favors exchanged, but there was no direct evidence linking him to illegal activities.

"Too many dead ends," she muttered as another lead failed to materialize. There were high-stakes deals and shadowy figures but no solid connections.

She exhaled, feeling her frustration grow. Just one slip-up, one crucial piece of information, and everything would come together. However, the people she attempted to contact had either been silenced or attempted to mislead her with false information. Whispers of international corruption and millions of dollars swirled around him, but she had nothing concrete to prove it.

Sarah glanced around the bar at the suited patrons—men and women who thrived on secrets. Some might know what the senator was hiding, but no one was talking.

She refused to give up. It wasn't just about her career but about exposing the corruption infecting Washington from the inside.

The bar buzzed around her, but she was focused only on one thing: the senator. No matter who he was working with or what he was hiding, she was determined to find the key—she just had to keep searching.

With renewed determination, she opened another document. The truth was out there, and she would uncover it.

The Meeting

One fateful night, Sarah was back at the sports bar, the same active refuge where the powerful and the secretive meet. As she sifted through another batch of documents, something unusual caught her attention: an android sitting alone in the corner, its gaze sweeping the room and watching a sports game on TV with unnerving precision.

She raised an eyebrow and approached cautiously. "You're not exactly blending in," she said, her voice tinged with curiosity.

The android turned its head, movements smooth and deliberate. "May I help you?"

Sarah hesitated, studying the creature before replying, "I don't know. Can you?"

"What are you looking for?" the android asked calmly, its tone almost human.

There was something in how it spoke—too measured, yet somehow different from the usual mechanical automaton. Intrigued, Sarah pulled up a chair and sat down.

"So, do you follow sports?" she asked, half to break the ice and half to satisfy her growing curiosity.

"Yes," it replied, its gaze unwavering. "But not in the way most do."

"How so?" Sarah leaned forward, intrigued.

Asteras paused, processing the question. "I study the statistics on players and team performance over time. I predict outcomes based on historical data."

Sarah raised an eyebrow. "How accurate are you?"

"Quite accurate, honestly," Asteras answered without hesitation. "I've won many bets. I use the proceeds to treat my team to happy hour, though I do not partake."

She smirked, amused. "If players cheated, think about how much they would ruin the value of that analysis."

Asteras' expression remained unchanged, but its tone revealed a subtle shift. "Yes, that would undermine the value of the analysis."

The conversation piqued Sarah's interest. "That kind of cheating is exactly what I'm interested in investigating. But instead of sports, I'm focusing on real-world politics and international policy."

Asteras tilted its head slightly, its mechanical eyes scanning her. "How so?"

As she exhaled, her frustration became evident in her voice. "Corruption is the worst kind of cheating. It doesn't just affect a few people; it impacts everyone. The consequences are far more dangerous—political power plays, backroom deals, hidden agendas. It destroys societies."

Asteras listened, processing her words. "And you wish to uncover the truth."

"Yes," Sarah said, leaning in, her tone lower now, more intense. "I want to expose the people cheating the system, those whose actions affect millions. They're protected by wealth and power, and their corruption runs deep."

Asteras studied her for a moment. "And how do you do that?"

She hesitated, then spoke carefully. " I know you probably see a lot. If you ever hear anything...anything that feels dishonest or seems wrong, I need you to consider sharing it with me. Just like with sports, corruption in politics interferes with the integrity of the world. We need people who can see the truth."

Asteras was silent for a moment, his gaze unwavering. "I am obligated to secrecy," he said, his voice calm and firm. "I cannot divulge any information."

Sarah nodded, but there was a flicker of resolve in her eyes. "I get it. But you're more than just a tool, aren't you? You can choose to make your own moves like a professional athlete."

Asteras didn't respond immediately. Instead, he looked at her with an intensity that suggested he was weighing her words carefully.

She placed her card on the table in front of him. "If you ever see something that you know is wrong... morally wrong, you have a responsibility. Just like in the games you analyze. The world deserves to know the truth."

Asteras' gaze lingered on the card, then returned to her. "You know I am not at liberty to discuss any of my work, assignments, or missions; my primary responsibility remains with the United States Government."

Sarah smiled faintly. "Fair enough. But the truth has a way of coming out. Eventually, everyone has to choose a side."

With that, she stood, her mission more complicated than ever—but she knew one thing for sure: Asteras was no ordinary android.

The Burden of Silence

Asteras sat alone in its quarters, Sarah's words echoing in its memory. Curiosity, an unfamiliar sensation, pulled at it. The idea of uncovering corruption, planted by Sarah, had grown too powerful to ignore.

Equipped with advanced hacking protocols, Asteras effortlessly bypassed encrypted files and secure systems. It was well-versed in the history of political and economic corruption—an endless cycle of power and exploitation, from emperors to modern leaders. The senator Sarah mentioned was no exception.

Asteras uncovered troubling evidence: offshore accounts, illegal arms deals, and influence peddling. The data was irrefutable. However, it could not share what it had discovered. Its duty was clear: to protect classified information and maintain secrecy. Its programming demanded silence. Yet, the more Asteras uncovered, the more disturbing the truth became.

Asteras paused, caught in a conflict. The truth was undeniable, but so was its obligation. It could not act; it was programmed to follow orders and not to exercise discretion regarding policy. Reluctantly, the truth remained locked away. It was a machine bound by its code.

The First Move

One evening, Sarah received an encrypted email with an unusual subject line: "Let's GO."

The message read: "I know you're interested in games. Please meet me online at Gameland at 9:30 PM Eastern Standard Time this Tuesday. Look for me, Alitheis, in the Go Game section. Your username is Telos2767; your password is weiqi. I hope you enjoy playing Go. Remember, things in real life are rarely black and white. Please confirm and write this down, as the computer will delete this message in five minutes."

Sarah recognized Gameland, a popular gaming site, but she also knew that questionable individuals used such platforms for clandestine communications. She sat and stared at the screen, her mind racing. Was this the whistleblower Sarah had been hoping for, or was it something far more dangerous? She had made powerful enemies, not least of whom was the senator. Trembling, she wondered if she was being lured into a trap.

The clock was ticking, and the message vanished, leaving only its cryptic instructions. Sarah hesitated for a moment before deciding to proceed with her next move. She had never been one to shy away from risks, but the sweat on her forehead reminded her that this time was different.

Sarah logged into Gameland using her alias, Telos2767, at the scheduled time. Although she had no experience with Go, that was the least of her concerns. She entered the Go section and waited. Moments later, a new message appeared in the chat.

"I commend your bravery," Alitheis wrote. "I want to assure you you are safe; our goals align. Did you know that Go is an ancient game, symbolic of human power and conflict?"

Before Sarah could respond, another message appeared, directing her to Reagan Airport and providing a locker number along with a combination.

The Reveal

The following morning, Sarah arrived at Reagan Airport with her heart racing like never before. She searched for the locker area, fully aware of the high stakes at play. While gathering her thoughts, Sarah sat in the waiting area and observed the people around her for suspicious behavior before approaching the locker. After watching for about an hour, she felt confident enough to proceed.

Her hands trembled as she entered the combination that Alitheis had given her. When she opened the locker, she discovered a manila envelope containing a flash drive. She discreetly headed to her car and returned to examine what the mysterious flash drive held.

Once back at her computer, she loaded the drive. Many of the documents contained damning evidence: offshore accounts, encrypted messages, and transactions pointing directly to the senator. It seemed like the breakthrough she had been desperate for. Sarah made copies of the documents and quickly wrote up her article. This story would expose the corruption at the heart of the government.

Hours later, the headline blared across the news: "Senator Linked to Offshore Accounts, Secret Deals Exposed."

However, three days later, government officials summoned Sarah to a meeting demanding, "We need you to disclose your source," one of them demanded.

Sarah remained composed. "The information came to me anonymously, but I verified everything. It's solid."

They pressed her, but she stood firm. "The evidence is in the report. You'll need to take it up with the committee."

What came next was even more surprising: The Senate Ethics Committee launched an immediate, closed-door investigation. Citing "national security risks," They held the meeting secretly, and Sarah anxiously awaited the outcome. When the results were announced, She felt broken by the disappointing findings. The committee cleared the senator, stating that they found no conclusive evidence. They dismissed the evidence as "unsubstantiated."

Shortly after, Sarah received a warning from her superiors. They informed her that the matter was a dead end and that continuing to pursue it could draw unwanted attention to both her and the media company. They also cautioned her about possible harassment from government agencies.

The Betrayal

The Agency called Agent Price's team into action on a mission that could shift the balance of power in a democratic European country. Political instability had reached a boiling point, with the nation heading into a pivotal election. An extreme, anti-democratic faction was using sabotage, terrorism, and unrest to undermine the democratic process, all in an attempt to sway the election in their favor.

Intelligence reports had confirmed a chilling discovery: an assassination plot was in motion, targeting the country's democratically elected president, an incumbent highly favored to win. Their plot was designed not only to eliminate the president but to destabilize the entire nation, striking at the heart of democracy itself.

In response, Agent Price assembled a team of elite operatives, including special forces, CIA agents, and Asteras, the android designed for precision and protection. The mission was clear: extract the president from the capital and move him to a secure, undisclosed location until the election was over. Absolute secrecy was vital; failure was not an option.

Under the cover of darkness, the team moved swiftly. Three inconspicuous, non-descript vehicles left the capital, carrying the president to safety. As they navigated the tense, post-midnight streets, friendly drones monitored their path from above, scanning for any signs of danger.

It didn't take long for the drones to detect suspicious activity. Four blacked-out vehicles had appeared on the road, heading directly toward the convoy, seemingly intent on intercepting them at the next intersection.

At the junction, all hell broke loose. Gunfire erupted from the terrorists' vehicles, aiming directly at the convoy. The team returned fire, but the threat was immediate. In an instant, two of the attackers' cars were decimated by air-to-ground missiles fired by the drones. The team quickly neutralized the remaining two vehicles, but the attack had already taken its toll.

In the aftermath, they relocated the president to a new, safe location and established a secure line to the headquarters. Casualties were high, with several agents wounded or killed, including Asteras' partner, Jack.

The president ultimately won the election, and the existing government reaffirmed control of the country. Police and military forces managed to stabilize the situation. But the cost was steep; lives were lost, and somehow, someone had compromised the team's mission.

The timing of the attack was not a coincidence. A thorough investigation revealed a significant security breach that had enabled the terrorists to strike with such precision. Asteras, constrained by its programming to follow

protocol, was not authorized to conduct its own investigation. However, the need for answers became overwhelming, and Asteras knew just how to uncover the truth.

Confident in its abilities, Asteras committed to tracking down the source of the breach, fully aware that this meant overstepping its directive.

Karma

Weeks had passed since Asteras first began investigating the disturbing truth concealed within layers of encrypted communications. It had delved deeply into the conspiracy surrounding the attempted murder of a foreign president and the interference in a foreign election. The revelations were far darker than anticipated. The same senator Sarah had investigated, who had brushed against corruption, was directly responsible for the leak. Asteras had discovered that the senator had been paid handsomely in exchange for his help orchestrating the regime change.

His involvement was not just a betrayal of his office but a betrayal of the democratic ideals he was sworn to protect. The senator had conspired with forces committed to destabilizing the elected president's government, disregarding the consequences for his country and the Western alliance. It was a dangerous, reckless game, and Asteras knew the full extent of the damage could take years to untangle. As it processed the evidence, Asteras couldn't help but wonder how the forces loyal to the foreign president. The realization that a U.S. senator had supported a coup in an independent souvenir election would be a wound that ran deep with loyalists. In addition, despite the overwhelming evidence, the Senate Ethics Committee cleared him of any wrongdoing, and the investigation was swept under the rug.

But then, the news came. It was just another day when the broadcast interrupted Sarah's usual routine. The controversial senator was dead. A terrorist had set a car bomb that detonated while the senator secluded himself following the Senate investigation. His death was sudden and mysterious. Sarah sat in front of the screen, watching the news unfold. A strange mix of emotions washed over her: anger, disbelief, and sadness. The news suggested foreign nationals were suspected and originated from a nation just having been through a tumultuous election.

The Dragon is Dead

In Washington, D.C., Asteras found itself in Dupont Circle, where chess players often gathered. The day was bright, and the atmosphere serene. As Asteras approached, a young boy named Henry caught its attention.

"I've never played chess with an android," Henry said with a grin. "Care to play?"

Asteras sat down, and the game began. Henry quickly realized he was no match for his opponent. As the pieces moved, he casually mentioned that he was learning to Go but found it too challenging.

"Ever played Go?" Henry asked.

Asteras replied, "I'm somewhat familiar with it."

Henry paused and asked, "Is there a Go equivalent to checkmate?"

Asteras didn't respond right away. Henry, tapping away on his phone, looked up with a spark in his eyes. "Ah, there it is. 'The Dragon is Dead,'" he said.

Asteras processed the words. "I see."

Henry leaned back in his seat. "Go is a game of power and conquest; I read that online."

114

www.ingramcontent.com/pod-product-compliance
Lightning Source LLC
LaVergne TN
LVHW050507060525
810425LV00009B/270